"You must think ... worldly…"

Rosanna nodded. "I can't understand how it's okay to have these things here, but it's a sin to have them in my former church."

"Yeah, I know," Zach said. "It doesn't make much sense, does it?"

"Who's wrong? The leaders in the Miller Amish, where I came from, or the leaders here?"

"You know we're not supposed to ask those questions," he reminded.

"I know, but why? I want to understand."

He smiled and stared at her in silence.

"What?" She smiled.

"You, that's what."

She shrugged. "I don't get it."

"You're beautiful."

Had she heard him right? "What?"

"I think you heard me." He grinned

She shook her head. "I don't know what you're talking about."

"I do."

She abruptly stood. "I think I better go inside."

"Don't."

"No, I need to." And she rushed through the door without glancing back.

By the grace of God, **J.E.B. Spredemann** resides in beautiful Southern Indiana Amish country and writes Christian fiction. May these books uplift you, inspire you, make you laugh and touch your heart. The author can be contacted via email at jebspredemann@gmail.com.

A SECRET
SACRIFICE

J.E.B. Spredemann

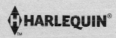

Recycling programs
for this product may
not exist in your area.

ISBN-13: 978-1-335-00601-1

A Secret Sacrifice

Copyright © 2017 by Jennifer Spredemann

This edition published by arrangement with Harlequin Books S.A.

For questions and comments about the quality of this book,
please contact us at CustomerService@Harlequin.com.

Printed in U.S.A.

Author's Note

It should be noted that the Amish/Mennonite people and their communities differ one from another. There are, in fact, no two Amish communities exactly alike. It is this premise on which this book is written. We have taken cautious steps to ensure the authenticity of Amish practices and customs. Old Order Amish and New Order Amish may be portrayed in this work of fiction and may differ from some communities.

We, as *Englischers,* can learn a lot from the Plain People and their simple way of life. Their hard work, close-knit family life and concern for others are to be applauded. As the Lord wills, may this special culture continue to be respected and remain so for many centuries to come, and may the light of God's salvation reach their hearts.

Unofficial Glossary
of Pennsylvania Dutch Words

Ach—Oh

Aldi—Girlfriend

Boppli—Baby

Bruder—Brother

Dat, Daed—Dad

Denki—Thanks

Der Herr—The Lord

Die Heilige Schrift—The Holy Script (Sacred Text, Holy Scriptures, German Luther Holy Bible)

Dochder—Daughter

Dummkopp—Dummy

Englischer—A non-Amish person

Ferhoodled—Mixed-up, crazy

Fraa—Woman, wife

Gott—God

Grossmudder—Grandmother

Gut—Good

Jah—Yes

Kinner—Children

Kinskinner—Grandchildren

Lieb (Liebchen)—Love, my love

Maed—Girls

Mamm—Mom

Nee—No

Newehocker—Side sitter (wedding attendant)

Ordnung—Rules of the Amish community

Schatzi—Sweetheart

Vatter—Father

Prologue

Zachariah Zook reached for the camouflage backpack adjacent to his thigh.

"Take cover! Now!" his comrade yelled as he dived behind their temporary fortress.

Zach's gaze shot toward where Jones' voice announced the command. He glanced toward an abandoned building, spotted the enemy, and hastily crawled toward their makeshift sandbag wall, dragging his pack with him. A pop, pop, pop sound told him they were being fired upon.

He buried his head in the cocoon of his muscled biceps, compliments of growing up on an Amish farm, while sand flew from enemy fire. *If only Bishop Hershberger could see me now.* He shook his head, dispelling thoughts of home.

Who knew if he'd even make it out of here alive? This was no time to lose his focus. There was a mission to accomplish—sneak in undetected, rescue the civilian refugees, and return home alive. But return to what? Hadn't he sacrificed everything to come here? When he returned, there wouldn't be a parade in his honor like there would be for the other soldiers. There would be no loved ones with balloons or signs welcoming him home. *Stop it!*

"Farm Boy? You okay?" Jones called.

Zach ignored his question. He listened in silence until fire from the enemy ceased. Rapid footsteps told him the enemy had moved on. Perhaps they hadn't been spotted after all. "Do you think they'll be back?"

"Most likely, but it looks like they've moved on for now. I hear the Humvee coming." Jones crawled toward him. "Your leg looks like it's bleeding. Did you get hit?"

Zachariah looked down. Sure enough, there was a flow of crimson soaking the canvas pant leg at his ankle.

Jones cursed under his breath. "Quick, let's bind that up so you don't bleed to death."

To death? He certainly wasn't ready to die, not with the rift between him and the church.

"I'm fine. I didn't even feel anything." Of course, after surviving a tractor accident, most pain never fazed him. He was no pansy.

"Nevertheless, it's our job to look out for each other." Jones pushed Zach's pant leg up and winced. He pulled out a bandana from his pants pocket and wrapped it around his ankle tightly. "It looks pretty bad. One of the medics will have to treat it when we get back to the barracks. I don't have the proper supplies."

That was his fault. If they had stayed with the other

troops, none of this would have happened and they'd possess whatever supplies they needed. "Sorry, man."

"No time for apologies. Here comes Peters. Let's go." Jones looked back at him. "Here, put your arm around me. I don't think you can walk on that."

Zach stood up and attempted to put pressure on his wounded leg. Excruciating pain shot through his entire body and he thought he might pass out. He breathed heavily and quickly grasped on to Jones. "I don't know what I'd do without you. Thanks." He forced the words through gritted teeth.

Jones nodded with a frown. "You gonna be okay?"

"I think so." A relieved sigh escaped Zach's lips as the Humvee finally approached, but he didn't eagerly anticipate the tongue lashing he was sure to receive from his superior. It wouldn't be any worse than the bishop's rebuke, would it?

Even so, he couldn't wait to get back home.

Chapter One

Anticipation twisted Rosanna Keim's fingers as the twelve-passenger van she rode in rolled to an abrupt stop. They'd arrived. She sighed as she thought about all the work that lay ahead of her and her family—not that they were strangers to hard work by any means. But *Dat*, although still strong as an ox, was getting up in years. Would the task before him prove too demanding on his aging body?

"Come, Rosanna," *Mamm* beckoned from the van door.

Her eyes roamed the vehicle. Was she the only one still inside? Had she been daydreaming that long?

"*Ach*, coming, *Mamm*." She clutched her book and the canvas bag at her feet and scurried out of the vehicle.

"And this," *Dat* announced, "Is our youngest, Rosanna."

She looked up to discover the family they'd be lodging with until their house was suitable to live in. The Zooks.

"Hello," she managed. As heat crept up her neck, she felt like her face needed a cool splashing of water from the creek. Meeting strangers always yanked her out of her comfort zone.

Her father continued. "Rosanna, this is Abram and Elnora, with their *kinner*, Zachariah, Benjamin, Elijah, Julia, and Loretta."

She forced herself to lift her eyes from her shoes and greet their hosts. "*Gut* to meet you."

"This will be your new teacher this year." Abram Zook gestured her way.

Rosanna smiled at the two youngest, who would presumably be her scholars. The boys, or young men rather, were surely too old to still be in school.

Did the oldest son just wink at her or had it been her imagination?

Elnora Zook stepped forward. "Come, let's go inside and get y'all settled. I'm sure you'd like to rest from your long journey." She looked to her sons. "Boys, please bring in the suitcases."

Rosanna followed her hostess into their home, but not without first taking a gander at their property. The rolling hills and thick woods surrounding the expansive farm created a thrill unlike any she'd ever known. What would it be like to explore the lush landscape? Were there any hidden caves, like the ones she'd read about before coming here?

Kentucky was certainly a beautiful state, stomach-churning hills and curves, notwithstanding. She didn't know how she'd ever get accustomed to driving in them. Fortunately, a horse and buggy traveled at a much slower pace than the fast-moving vehicle she'd emerged from a few moments ago. Perhaps it wouldn't be as bad as she thought it would.

"Mary, you and Isaac may use this bedroom." Elnora walked to a door past the kitchen and whisked it open. "And girls," she looked to Rosanna and her two sisters, "this is your room." She opened a door just beyond the room her parents would be sleeping in.

Rosanna peered inside to see a set of bunk beds and a full-sized bed. The room was simple, but clean.

"I'll leave you three to get settled." Their hostess stepped out of the room and lightly closed the door behind her.

"You get the bottom, Rosanna," Frances said, claiming the top bunk as her own. "I wish I was the oldest so I could have the big bed."

"Well, you're not, so too bad," her sister Margaret teased.

Rosanna noticed a door on the opposite wall. She knocked on it but didn't hear anyone on the other side. Should she open it? She pulled the knob gently and smiled in surprise. "Look, we have a bathroom."

Both sisters rushed over to peek inside.

"I bet that door goes to *Mamm* and *Dat's* room. We'll have to remember to lock both sides when we use it," Margaret said.

"It has a shower!" Frances beamed. "This sure beats our outhouse back home. Do you think *Dat* will put a shower in our new place or will we still have to use a wash tub?"

"We'll have to ask him." Rosanna turned when she heard a knock on the door to their room.

"Answer that," Margaret commanded.

Rosanna walked to the door and pulled it open.

"Your bags have arrived." Zachariah wriggled his eyebrows over the top of three suitcases. "Where would you like them?"

"I'll take this one." Rosanna reached for the uppermost suitcase. "You can just set the others down."

"Okie dokie. *Mamm* said to tell you supper should be ready around five."

As he set the luggage down, Rosanna's eyes immediately noticed how his shirt strained over his upper arms. She quickly looked away. "*Denki.*"

Zachariah nodded, and then disappeared in short order.

Rosanna closed the door.

"He likes you," Margaret teased.

Rosanna gasped. "He does not."

"I think he does too," Frances chimed in.

"Stop it. Both of you," Rosanna warned.

"Well, that *is* why *Mamm* and *Dat* wanted to move here, to get us married off," Margaret snickered.

"That's not true." Rosanna shook her head. "I'm only seventeen and I plan to teach for a long time. I certainly am not looking for a boyfriend."

Frances smiled, ignoring her words. "It looks like you'll be first."

Zachariah stared at the ceiling. The tick-tock from his clock didn't help his insomnia. He reached over and grasped his flashlight and shined it on the clock. Twelve. He should have been asleep for two hours already. Why couldn't he sleep?

He knew. It was her.

For some reason, he hadn't expected the Keim girls to be pretty. No, not pretty. Rosanna was gorgeous. With hair the color of chocolate with streaks of gold running through it, and striking hazel eyes, she was probably the most beautiful girl he'd ever seen. And since she was to be the new teacher, that meant she was intelligent. And probably kind too. If you worked with children, you had to be kind. He wondered if she had any idea how beautiful she was. She'd probably had boys lined up outside her door in Indiana.

Supper had been torture. He'd done his best to divert his gaze, but had failed miserably. There was something about her that drew him to her, like a bear drawn to a honeycomb. She had been quiet during the meal, while her sisters chatted about anything and everything. He wondered what she'd been thinking about. Certainly not about him.

He heaved a sigh and pushed his covers off. He'd never get any sleep at this rate.

He reached for his pants and pulled the suspenders over his chest. Maybe some fresh air would do him some good. He quietly tiptoed down the stairs and walked out onto the porch. Fortunately, their guest quarters were at the opposite end of the house and they wouldn't be disturbed by his restlessness.

The sky was clear tonight with nary a cloud as far as his eyes could see. He stepped out onto the blanket of cool grass, and reveled in the satisfaction this simple activity afforded. Walking barefoot had always been a favorite pastime. Somehow, it managed to clear his head and bring a peace of sorts.

The wind whirled through the ancient trees surrounding their property and the fresh breeze brought on a slight shiver. Perhaps he should have grabbed his shirt as well. He stepped back onto the porch to avoid the crisp breeze. He moved toward the porch swing then abruptly stopped in his tracks.

"Rosanna?"

Rosanna had kept silent as she'd watched Zachariah walk in the grass. She hadn't wished to startle him, but now she could keep silent no more.

"I couldn't sleep, so I came out to sit on the porch. I hope I didn't awaken you." It was a good thing it wasn't very bright outside, otherwise he'd have seen her blush. She wasn't used to seeing young men half dressed.

"No. I couldn't sleep either." He glanced down at his chest. "I guess I'll just go back inside."

"You don't have to on my account."

"You sure?"

She nodded then realized he probably couldn't see her. "*Jah*."

He sat on the swing next to her and she did her best to avert her eyes. Zachariah Zook was certainly easy to look at. Too easy. She briefly wondered if he had an *aldi*.

"So, what do you think of Kentucky so far?"

"*Ach*, I love it. It's so *schee*. Is it like this every night?"

"Has been lately, but I reckon it'll be gettin' cooler as the weather turns. I'm guessin' it's a little warmer here than northern Indiana."

"*Jah.* I think I'll really like the winters here."

"It's just the right amount of snow for me. Enough to have some fun, but not too much to keep you from goin' places."

"Is there enough for ice skating?" She thought of the exciting times she'd had out on their pond each year when it had frozen over. Her sisters and friends would stay out on the ice for as long as they could stand it, then they'd all make their way to the house to warm up by the fire and sip hot apple cider.

"Depends. Not every year. It doesn't always get cold enough for the ponds to freeze."

"I see."

"*Dat* and I went to see your farm the other day." He grimaced. "It looks like it's goin' to need a lot of work."

That's not what she wanted to hear. "I have yet to see it. How long has it been vacant for?"

"About four years now. That's when the Borntregers moved out. It tends to get pretty wet here, so the mildew has taken over some of the siding. Your *vatter* may have to replace some walls."

"I guess that's why the price was so low. But there's nothing hard work and determination can't fix, no?"

He nodded. "I think Bishop Hershberger has a frolic planned for next week. We should be able to knock out a lot of the heavy work then. You'll get to meet everyone at meeting this week. There'll be a gathering afterwards."

"Sounds like fun." Although she tended to be introverted for the most part, she looked forward to making new friends. Which reminded her, she needed to write a letter to Magdalena tomorrow. Did her friend miss her?

"Did you enjoy the singings in your former district?"

"*Jah*, but sometimes some of the *kinner* got a little wild. If you know what I mean." She frowned.

"Ya mean drinkin' and such?"

"And such." She nodded. "I don't believe in drinking. Do you?"

He scratched his head and her attention was immediately drawn to his brawny frame again. She forced herself to look away. "Well, I'd be lyin' if I said I've never had a drink. But I don't make it a practice, no."

"One of the boys in one of the wilder groups overdosed on drugs about a year ago." She shuddered, remembering the horrible day. "The leaders had some *Englischers* come in and talk to us young folks. Police officers. Not everyone was happy about it, but after Rudy died I think they just gave up fighting. No one wants to see their loved ones go through that."

"Did it help?"

"Some, I think. You know how willful some young people can be; sometimes nothing gets through to them."

"Tell me about your old district. How were they different from here?"

"Well, I'm still unsure of all the rules yet. But from what I can tell so far, this group is a lot faster."

"Really? I've heard stories about the Amish folks up north."

"Well, our group was pretty small so we didn't intermingle much with others."

"So, how are we faster?"

"You have bathrooms inside the house. And your buggies are fancier. We didn't have gas appliances either."

"No way. Wow! I bet this is a step up for you then."

"About three steps, I think." She laughed.

"So you must think we're pretty worldly."

She nodded. "I can't understand how it's okay to have these things here, but it's a sin to have them in my former church."

"Yeah, I know. It doesn't make much sense, does it?"

"Who's wrong? The leaders in the Miller Amish, where I came from, or the leaders here?"

"You know we're not supposed to ask those questions," he reminded.

"I know, but why? I want to understand."

He smiled and stared at her in silence.

"What?" She smiled.

"You, that's what."

She shrugged. "I don't get it."

"You're beautiful."

Had she heard him right? "What?"

"I think you heard me." He grinned.

She shook her head. "I don't know what you're talking about."

"I do." He leaned in and stole a quick kiss.

"*Ach*, Zachariah!"

"You can call me Zach."

"You…you kissed me."

"And?"

She abruptly stood up. "I think I better go inside."

"Don't." He reached for her hand.

"No, I need to." She rushed through the door without glancing back.

Chapter Two

Rosanna plunged her hands into the warm soapy water. What a blessing it was to turn on a faucet and have hot water at your fingertips in just a few seconds. She'd never known what she was missing back in Indiana. She knew there were *Englischers* who lived this way, but Amish? No, that was something she never could have imagined; it was way too modern for Amish. And yet, here she was.

"May I help?"

"Zachariah? *You* wash dishes?" She turned and looked at him. Fortunately, he was fully dressed today. But Zachariah Zook looked good either way, she admitted to herself.

He lifted a handsome grin. "Sometimes."

Rosanna looked behind her to be sure neither of her sisters were nearby. The last thing she wanted was to invite more teasing from her sisters. Their voices outside told her they were most likely hanging laundry. "Sure, if you'd like to."

"I can dry them and put them away."

She nodded.

He picked up a hand towel and began drying the glassware. "So, she's beautiful, smart, and hard workin'. Those are some good qualities to possess."

"And what is he?" She glanced his way as she wiped the dish with her rag and then dropped it into the rinse water.

"You tell me," he challenged.

"Well, I don't really know him too well."

"We can change that." He reached into the rinse water and lightly brushed her fingers with his.

She knew her cheeks must be flaming. Zachariah Zook was certainly too fast of a young man to date for her liking. She moved her hand away. "I don't know."

"Why? Do you not find me attractive?"

Did he have to be so forthright? Surely, he knew he was handsome. "*Jah*, I find you attractive," she admitted. "But you're much too fast for me."

"Fast?"

"You've already kissed me, Zachariah Zook. Without invitation."

"Did you not enjoy it?"

"I think this conversation is over."

"Ah, so you *did* enjoy it." He grinned, obviously satisfied with his conclusion.

Rosanna dipped her hand into the water and flicked it at Zach.

"Is Rosanna Keim getting frustrated? I'll have to add feisty to that list of qualities." He rose to the challenge by splashing water back at her.

She looked down at the water spot on her apron and gasped. "You."

"I'm not done yet." He scooped up a handful of water and held it over her head.

"You wouldn't."

He let the water seep through his hand, then dumped the entire contents over her head. "Ha. Ha."

"I can't believe you just did that." She couldn't not retaliate; not after that. She brought both of her hands out of the rinse water and wiped them on his stubbly cheeks.

He grasped her hands and pulled her close. "Hey, I like your hands there," his husky voice caught her off-guard. He had her pinned between the counter and his body. "What if I kissed you right now?"

Her heartbeat quickened at his closeness. She wriggled under his stronghold, while simultaneously fighting a smile. "You wouldn't."

His brow rose and he stared longingly at her lips. "Wouldn't I?"

She bit her lower lip as she anticipated his inevitable kiss.

"Zachariah!"

He immediately let go and spun around at the sound of his father's voice.

"*Dat*, I—"

"Get outside at once." His father pointed to the back door and quickly followed his son outside. Zach was sure to get a talking to.

Rosanna turned back to the task at hand and sighed. Her feelings for Zach were very confusing. Could you like a person and dislike them at the same time? On the one hand, Zachariah Zook was handsome and charming and likeable. But on the other hand, he seemed persistent and headstrong and way too determined.

If she didn't watch herself, she could imagine a boy like Zachariah getting her into mischief. Perhaps it wasn't such a *gut* idea for them to be living under the same roof. *Jah*, she'd have to be certain sure to stay away from him as much as possible.

Rosanna held her nose as she gingerly walked through the tattered house. If she breathed in one more whiff of mildew, she was sure to have another sneezing spell. What on earth had her father been thinking when he signed on the dotted line to purchase this place? It would probably be better to tear the thing down and start fresh, in her opinion.

"Well, what do you think, daughter?" her father's chipper voice called from outside the window.

"Are you sure this is the right place?" she managed, releasing her breath for a moment.

"Come on outside," he beckoned.

Gladly. She came around the side of the house to meet her father.

He put his arm around her shoulders. "Oh, I know it doesn't look like much now, but you just wait."

Wait she would have to do. They wouldn't be moved in by Christmas at this rate. Could she bear to live in the same household with Zachariah Zook several more months? She certainly didn't think so.

He turned her to the trees facing south. "You see those trees there? Those are ours." He turned her to the east. "And those." Then to the west. "And those. Fifty acres, Rosie! And just look at this land. Plenty to raise a good crop with the best soil money can buy. There's a stream just beyond those trees where we can fish. And did you see the deer grazing in the meadow when we pulled up to the house? It's practically Heaven!"

It was hard not to catch her father's infectious enthusiasm. But Heaven? "Where's the mansion?" she jested.

"Oh, stop." He gestured to the house. "I know it isn't much, but we'll get it livable before we move in."

"How long will it take?"

"Well, I plan to come and work on it every day. Abram said his boys would be happy to help. I'm thinking it'll be livable in a month."

"Really?"

"Or less." He patted her back.

She sighed in relief.

His brow arched half an inch. "What's wrong? Don't you like staying with the Zooks? They have a nice place."

"Shh…they'll hear you." She peered around the corner.

His hand waved her concern away. "Nah. They're over on the other side of the property. I think they walked down to the creek."

"Their place is very nice. It's not that."

His knowing grin gave him away. "It's the oldest boy, isn't it?"

She remained silent.

"I thought he had an eye for you." He faced her and held her gaze. "Do you need me to run him off?"

"*Nee, Dat.* That's not necessary."

"Well, you let me know if it *becomes* necessary. Okay?"

She nodded.

Zachariah raised his chainsaw and proceeded to cut through the log he and Benjamin had hauled out of their woods this morning. At the rate he was going today, he'd soon have cut enough wood for two winters. It didn't matter, though. He enjoyed cutting wood and *Dat* would certainly appreciate the abundance. It helped him get his mind off things. Usually.

He did his best not to think about the other night on the porch with Rosanna. Nor of their kitchen rendezvous, which his father not-so-gently let him know was not acceptable. What on earth had he been thinking? She'd been avoiding him like the plague ever since and he certainly deserved it. *Dummkopp.* Yep, he'd blown it for sure and certain. He now wondered if he'd ever get the chance to apologize for his untoward behavior.

He glanced toward the house, where Rosanna now hung laundry with her sister. Too bad she wasn't alone.

He brought another log close and sliced through it like his *Mamm's* delicious homemade bread. Before long, he had a good size pile and he stacked it all neatly in the woodshed. When he walked out, he looked toward the laundry line again. Was Rosanna alone now?

"Rosanna," he called out.

She clipped a sheet to the laundry line, then looked over.

"Come here." He motioned for her to meet him.

She looked hesitant, but eventually began walking toward him.

Good.

She stopped several feet away. "I don't have anything to say to you."

"I don't think that's true. Anyway, I do have somethin' I need to say to you." He took a few steps toward her, closing the gap between them.

She fidgeted and glanced back toward the house. "I have work to do."

He reached out and grasped her arm. "Wait. Just a minute, please."

She pulled her arm away.

"Rosanna, is there a problem?"

Zachariah spun around at the sound of her father's voice. Where had he come from? Why could they never get an uninterrupted moment alone?

Zachariah spoke up. "No, sir. We were just talking."

Her father frowned. "I was talking to my daughter. Last I checked, you weren't her."

Did Rosanna just stifle a laugh? *Now I really feel like an idiot.*

"It's okay, *Dat*. I was just going back to my laundry." With that, she turned and walked back to resume the task she'd left.

Her father eyed him warily. "Zachariah, I appreciate your family allowing us to stay here and the help you've given on the house. However, I will not tolerate my daughters being taken advantage of."

What had she told him?

"Do I make myself clear?"

Zachariah nodded.

"Good, we have an understanding. You may continue with your work." With that, Isaac Keim walked off.

Zachariah walked back to the wood he'd been stacking and kicked the log in front of him, but the pain in his toe didn't outweigh the regret now churning in his soul. He'd really blown it this time.

Dear Magdalena,
Greetings in the name of our Lord!
I must say that moving to Kentucky has been quite an adventure! I really like it here so far.
We haven't met too many people yet, just the family we're staying with—the Zooks. They seem really nice. They have three boys and two girls. The two girls are the youngest and they will be my scholars. I think the oldest boy, Zachariah, likes me. He's friendly, or too friendly, I should say. Between you and me, I think he's quite handsome. I know what you're thinking but don't go getting carried away with your ferhoodled *romantic ideas. I don't see myself dating Zach, he's much too confident of himself for my taste.*
You should see the place that Dat *purchased— or maybe you shouldn't? It's pretty bad. The house, I mean. It needs A LOT of work and it wonders me if we wouldn't be better off just tearing it down and building a new one.* Dat *thinks it will be ready to move into within a month, but I don't see how that's going to happen. The property itself is really pretty, though. We have all kinds of*

*woods and a stream. There are a few hills too, so
there's plenty to explore.*

*Honey Ridge is very different from Miller
Amish. The Zooks' house almost looks like it
could belong to an* Englischer. *They have two
bathrooms inside the house with a bathtub and
a shower! We can take several showers a week
if we have a mind to, although I don't know who
would need that many. And the water is fresh from
a well outside, so there is plenty. I no longer have
to get the last leftover water after everyone else
is done bathing—I get to use my own water. Let
me say that it feels really* gut. *Being the youngest
isn't so bad anymore.*

*I am certain sure you would love it here. Maybe
you can come visit sometime after our house is
finished with repairs. Summertime might be good
because I'll be out of school and I'll probably
have a little extra time.*

How is your family doing? Is your bruder
happy with his new fraa? *Please tell everyone
hello, especially your* grossmudder. *Write me
back soon!*

Your friend,
Rosanna

Rosanna stared at the quilt on her bed as she ran the
brush through her hair. She'd replayed the events of the
day in her mind several times now. What had Zachariah
been so eager to speak with her about? And what nerve
he had clutching her arm like that! Was he about to try

to kiss her again in broad daylight? Hadn't his father's earlier reprimand been enough? Surely, Zachariah Zook thought way too much of himself.

She almost chuckled aloud when she recalled his re-action to *Dat*. He sure did run Zachariah off *gut*. Serves him right, trying to force her attention like that.

"What are you smiling about, Rosie?" Margaret sat on her own bed braiding her hair.

"I bet she's thinking about meeting tomorrow," Frances chimed from the bunk above Rosanna's head. "I wonder if it'll be much different than back home."

"Probably," Rosanna said.

"Do you think there're any handsome boys here?" Frances crooned.

Rosanna thought of Zach then immediately averted her thoughts. She shrugged.

"I'm dreading the fact that everyone will probably be staring at us," Margaret moaned.

"Ah, it's okay. Maybe the boys will notice you then." Frances laughed.

Margaret plucked up her pillow and hurled it at her younger sister.

"Oh, good. I was hoping for an extra pillow," Frances teased.

Rosanna settled into bed and yawned. Sometimes, it seemed like she was the mature one out of the three. "Goodnight, sisters."

Margaret caught the pillow her sister flung back at her and turned the gas lamp down.

Soon Rosanna was off to a peaceful sleep despite the swarm of butterflies in her stomach.

Chapter Three

Rosanna clenched her apron between her fingers as the minister introduced her family to their new Amish congregation. Thank goodness, her sisters each sat at her side, otherwise she'd be overcome with anxiety. While she didn't mind teaching the scholars, being in the presence of a large room full of mostly adult strangers made her nervous. Especially since she could feel Zach's eyes glued to her. But it wasn't just him. Several of the other young Amish men seemed to look her way. It was times like this she wished she could just disappear with a good book or walk amongst nature. Alone.

Soon after the service had ended, the congregants began assembling benches to prepare for the common meal. Rosanna had already gotten a glimpse of the food they'd be partaking of and her stomach now grumbled. She briefly wondered if their peanut butter spread was as delicious as the one *Mamm* had taught her to make. The common meal was often her favorite time on Sundays. That, and returning to a peaceful home after the hullabaloo was over.

She quickly found her mother in the kitchen and busied herself with placing food on the tables. The women served the men, who typically ate first. She made a special effort to avoid the table that Zachariah and many of the young men occupied. When the simple meal was placed on the table in its entirety—sliced bread, bologna, cheese, peanut butter spread, pickled beets, and other canned goods most likely the bounty from this year's harvest—Rosanna found the table her sisters sat at and joined them.

"Do you mind if we sit here?"

Rosanna looked to the possessor of the feminine voice and smiled. "That's fine."

"Hi, I'm Lizzie and this is my sister, Patricia. Seems we're about the same age, ain't so?"

"I'm seventeen," Rosanna volunteered.

"Nineteen," Frances said. "And Margaret's twenty-one."

"I'm eighteen," Lizzie said. "Patricia's twenty."

Patricia grinned. "Are y'all comin' to the gathering tonight?"

"It'll be here, *jah*?" Rosanna asked.

Lizzie nodded. "At six."

"Of course, we will!" Frances answered for everyone.

The quiet room, aside from Margaret's soft snore, should have been conducive for a good nap. But Rosanna couldn't sleep even if her life depended on it. She really should get some rest before the young folks' gathering tonight. She turned over, squeezed her eyes shut, and attempted to force herself to sleep.

It was no use.

She lifted herself from the bed, removed her prayer *kapp* from the hook on the wall, and tiptoed out of her shared room. Maybe a nice walk would do her some good. If it didn't tire her out enough for a nap, hopefully it would at least calm her nerves for the evening ahead.

As she walked toward the barn, she noticed an unfamiliar buggy parked at the Zooks' hitching post. Did the Zooks have company? She glanced back toward the house but saw no one. She took a few more steps and heard two voices, male voices. One was Zachariah's.

Should she continue on her planned path past the barn and into the woods? What if she interrupted an important conversation? She listened closer. Zach and whoever it was must've been in the barn.

Rosanna ignored them and began to walk toward the woods—that was when she heard her name. She stopped cold.

"Do you think she'll ride home with me tonight?" An unfamiliar voice asked.

"I don't know, John. Rosanna's pretty, but she seems kind of stuck on herself to me," Zach said.

Rosanna gasped. *How dare he!*

"Will you ask her for me?" John asked.

"Are you kidding? She won't give me the time of day. I'm afraid you'll have to ask her yourself."

"Never mind. I'll have my sister ask for me."

"Hey, I'm sorry, man. I really wouldn't mind, but I don't think her father cares for me much."

"*Why not? You're a nice enough guy.*"

"*I tried to talk to her the other day, but before I could even say anything, her* daed *ran me off.*"

"*Why would he do that?*"

"*Who knows?*"

"*You don't think he'd be against me driving her home from the singing, do you? I mean, why would he allow her to go in the first place if she's not allowed to date?*"

"*Well, maybe it's just because she's the youngest of the three sisters. I don't know. I can't figure them out.*"

Rosanna rolled her eyes. Zach knew good and well why she avoided him.

She determined then and there that whoever this John guy was, she would ride with him tonight. If for no other reason than to put Zachariah in his place. And she'd do her utmost to prove Zachariah wrong. How could he say she was stuck up when he didn't even know her? She'd show him. If anyone was stuck on himself, it was surely Zachariah Zook.

Zachariah knew this would happen. As soon as his friends laid their eyes on Rosanna, they'd want to court her. Of course, he had too. But he wasn't about to tell John that. His attempts at changing his friend's mind didn't work. He knew John didn't care for *maed* that thought they were all that, so he tried to use that angle. But John didn't even seem to care when it came to Rosanna.

If it had been anyone other than his best friend, he would have told them to back off. But since it was John, he gave in. They'd been best friends since the first day of school when they sat next to each other in class. He'd barely known John's family from seeing them at meeting every other week. The boys would play together sometimes, but John had mostly stayed close to his older brothers. John had been more timid than Zachariah, probably because Zach had been an older sibling. But that first day of school, they'd hit it off and the rest, as they would say, was history.

Good friends were hard to come by and Zach was determined not to let anything come between them. Not even beautiful Rosanna.

Angst filled Rosanna as she walked toward the barn where she was to meet John. If her sisters hadn't been there tonight, she probably would have stayed home. Just knowing that she was going to be riding home with a young man—a stranger, at that—caused her nerves to jumble.

John's sister had pointed him out to Rosanna, so at least she knew what he looked like. He'd been one of the handsome young men eyeing her during the meeting. She'd already kind of figured which one he might be because he and Zachariah spoke often throughout the evening. She briefly wondered how well he and Zach knew each other.

She now waited for John's buggy to emerge from the barn.

"Ready?"

She turned at John's voice and paused in surprise. Though she hadn't noticed at a distance, up close John had a remarkable resemblance to Zach. They shared dark hair, blue eyes, and a medium build, though John seemed to be a little less stocky and had a softer, more pleasant face, as though he was always ready to laugh.

"Uh, *jah*." She stepped up onto the side of the buggy and hoisted herself onto the cushioned seat.

John made a kissing sound and gently slapped the reins to get the driving horse moving.

"Hi." John glanced her way and smiled.

"Hi."

"I'm John Christner."

"Rosanna Keim." She nodded. This was the first time she'd ever ridden with a complete stranger, so meeting this way seemed a bit odd.

"So, tell me about yourself, Rosie. You don't mind if I call ya Rosie, do you?"

Rosanna smiled. "*Nee*. My *vatter* sometimes calls me that." She turned toward him. "What do you want to know?"

"How old are you?"

"Seventeen. And you?"

"Twenty-one."

"How many siblings do you have?"

"Hey, I thought I was the one asking the questions." His laugh came easy.

"We both are."

"A question thief she is. So that's how the game's played?" He offered her the reins. "Would you like to take these too?"

She could tell by his tone that he was teasing her, so she teased right back. "I think I will." She reached for the reins and he shook his head.

"I don't think so, Rosie. I don't know you well enough to let you drive just yet."

Rosanna laughed.

"Five," John said.

"Five, what?"

"So you have a bad memory too? Seems like a guy could use that to his advantage." He chuckled. "I have five siblings. Two sisters and three brothers."

"Older or younger?"

"Both. I'm the youngest of the boys. One older sister and one younger."

"I'm the youngest of three girls."

"The baby, huh?"

"I guess."

"So, that means you're spoiled then. I don't know how I feel about that."

"I should slap you for that."

"Oh, so you're violent too? Man, Zach really should've warned me."

"Have you ever considered becoming a comedian?"

He shook his head and tsked. "Rosie, Rosie, Rosie. You should know that a comedian is not a bishop-approved occupation."

"You know what? You're right. No one would come to your shows anyway."

"Ow. Now that wasn't nice."

"Who's the baby now?"

"Leave me alone. I'm still licking my wounds."

"Oh, boy."

He laughed, and then glanced her way. "On the serious side, where do you think we should go? If someone is bringing your sisters home, the Zooks' living room might be occupied."

She shrugged. "I don't know. I'm not from around here so I don't know what you hillbillies usually do for fun."

John hooted. "Well, I reckon yer right. Us'ns here in the sticks be havin' a hoedown somedays, unless yer aginit."

"Okay. You're either going to have to speak *Deitsch* or English because I have no idea what you just said." Rosanna laughed. "That accent was pretty good though. You sounded just like the older man at the gas station. I couldn't really understand him either."

"I'll take that as a compliment." He chuckled. "You do know what a hoedown is, right?"

Rosanna's lips twisted. "Dancing?"

"I guess it could include dancing. We just usually play instruments, though."

"Really?"

"Yeah."

"And that's allowed?"

John shrugged. "Ah, not really but we do it anyway."

"So you're a rebel?"

"And you're a Yankee?"

"Not exactly. And you know that's not what I meant."

"What did you mean, Rosie?"

"What happens if the bishop finds out? Or your folks? I would think that playing music wouldn't be an easy thing to hide."

"They already know. I suspect they did it too when

they were our age. It's all in fun. Ain't nothin' wrong with havin' a little fun, is there?"

"I reckon there ain't iffen yer folks know and don't do nothin' about it." She realized she probably sounded foolish trying out her accent but it was fun nonetheless.

"Hey, you sound kinda cute with a southern drawl. I think you northern folk might just make it out here in the sticks after all."

"So, where's this hoedown you've been talking about?"

"Ain't one planned for tonight. But I do have my harp."

"You play the harp?" She tried to reconcile the words harp and hoedown, but they didn't seem to mesh in her mind. For the life of her, she couldn't picture John playing a harp.

He reached into his pocket and handed her a rectangular box.

She opened it up. "It's a harmonica."

He nodded. "My mouth harp."

Now it made sense. He'd been referring to a harmonica. Now, *that* she could picture. "Can you play something?"

He handed her the reins and she held them steady while he played. The tune sounded a little familiar, but she couldn't tell what it was. When he finished the song, she handed the reins back.

"That was really nice."

"Did you like it?"

"I did. What was it?"

"It's called *O' Susanna*, but I was imagining the words to say O' Rosanna."

"I hope it has good words."

"It's just an old folk song. Mostly just for fun." He slipped the harmonica back into his pocket. "We can just drive around tonight. Or we can drive by the Zooks' and see if there are any extra buggies there."

"That's fine."

"You don't mind going back to the Zooks' place, do you?"

"You don't think they'll be up still?"

"Probably not. If someone is there, we can just hang out in the buggy and talk."

"That sounds *gut*."

"Any idea when your folks' place will be ready?"

She grimaced. "Between you and me, I don't know if we'll ever move out of the Zooks' place."

"That bad, huh?"

"I think it would probably be better to tear the place down and build a new house."

"Well, I'd be willing to help out with whatever's needed. I enjoy construction. Things are beginning to slow down on the farm and I'll have extra time."

"That's kind of you to offer. I'll let my father know. He's been out there every day. Except for today, of course."

"I enjoy working with wood and building things. Someday soon, I'd like to start on my own place. I already have money saved up for a piece of property."

"That's *gut*."

John guided the driving horse into the Zooks' long

tree-lined lane. "I've always loved this driveway. This place is somewhat like a hideaway, *ain't so*?"

"*Jah*. I think that's why my *vatter* was so excited to move out here. All the hills and trees and such. I've read about the caves they have out here. Have you ever been to any of them?"

"Not the famous ones. But the Millers have one on their property. It's not very big, but amazing nonetheless."

Rosanna didn't try to tamper her enthusiasm. "Really? I've always wanted to see a cave."

"I could take you."

"You would?"

"Yeah, sure." He smiled, then turned to her. "You're not afraid of bats, are you?"

"Bats?" She swallowed.

"*Jah*. They pretty much mind their own business as long as they don't get riled up. One time, Zach and I made the mistake of disturbing them. It's a lesson I won't forget too soon, that's for sure and certain." He laughed. "I don't think I've ever run so fast in my life. I could have sworn one of them bit my neck, but we couldn't find any evidence of it afterward."

"That's scary."

"I don't think you have to worry, though. They're usually just sleeping in there. And if they were to get riled up for some reason, I'd protect you."

"You would?"

"Of course."

"*Denki*."

He nodded, and silence briefly filled the buggy.

"Well, it's getting late. I should probably let you go now. I forgot. You start school tomorrow, right?"

"*Jah*. It's just going to be an orientation. I'll actually begin teaching on Tuesday."

"Rosie?"

"*Jah*?"

"I had a *gut* time getting to know you tonight."

"Me too."

"Would you… I mean, it's probably too soon to ask you to court me only. Will you ride home with me at the next gathering?"

"I'd like that." Rosanna smiled.

"You would?" His brow shot up in apparent surprise.

"Very much."

"*Wunderbaar*! Okay, then. I'll see you then if not sooner."

"*Guten nacht*, John." Her eyes met his and he held her gaze for several seconds.

A smile danced on his lips. "Good night, Rosanna."

Rosanna could hear John's contented whistle as he traveled down the Zooks' majestic lane. She couldn't wipe the silly schoolgirl smile off her lips. *Jah, this was a gut evening.* She couldn't help but wonder if John might be the one. Only time would tell.

Chapter Four

The day had finally arrived. *This* was the day Rosanna had been looking forward to since moving. Her first day of school in Honey Ridge. She'd only be observing today as the resigning teacher, a young woman who'd recently married and was now expecting, showed her the ropes. She wondered how different teaching school in Honey Ridge would be compared to the school she taught at in her former district.

The memories of her former scholars were bittersweet. She'd loved teaching, but a few of the students proved to be a handful at times. Hopefully, the children in Honey Ridge would be more respectful. Teaching was a joy when children desired learning, but when they had no interest whatsoever was when it became difficult. She'd done her best to be positive about it, but still the difficulties remained.

After church yesterday, she'd met with the leaders briefly. Because she was to be the new teacher, and therefore a mentor to her scholars, they'd asked her to conform to the district's dress mandates already. Since she hadn't had time to sew her own dresses, she'd be borrowing a couple from the deacon's daughter. Elnora Zook had been generous to offer the use of one of her *kapps* until Rosanna had time to make her own. Fortunately, *Mamm* said she'd be sewing a couple of dresses and *kapps* for Rosanna this week, since she'd be busy with school.

Although it had only been her first day, it was easy to see which students enjoyed school and which ones simply endured it. Julia and Loretta, Zachariah's sisters, seemed to do well and abided by the rules. She'd expected them to since they usually behaved well at home—at least, when their older brothers weren't teasing them. And that made Rosanna wonder what Zach had been like in school. A handful, most likely. And there was no doubt in her mind that John Christner had probably been quite the mischief maker too. Partners in crime, those two must've been.

Rosanna's cheery countenance over the last few days had nearly driven Zach crazy. She'd seemed almost blissful since Monday morning and he wondered if her date with John had anything to do with it. Who was he kidding? It had *everything* to do with it.

If he'd been smart, he would have told his best friend that *he* sought to court her. He should have known that they'd hit it off. Who could resist John's quick wit and charm? He could kick himself for being such a *dummkopp*. How on earth was he going to keep himself away from his best friend's girl—if that was indeed what she was?

Perhaps he should pay John a visit to see if he'd share anything about their date. What on earth had his friend said or done to make Rosanna fall for him so quickly?

Or maybe Rosanna's demeanor had nothing to do with John whatsoever. Could she be this excited because she'd started teaching school? Females had always been a peculiar mystery to him and that was something he didn't think he'd ever understand. Nevertheless, a visit to John was in order.

"Hey, Zach, how ya doin'?" John looked up at him from under the buggy.

"Pretty *gut*. We've been making a lot of headway on the Keims' house." He scratched the stubble on his chin. "What are you doing under there?"

"There was some rattling noise and I'm trying to figure out where it's coming from." He slid out from under the carriage. "That's great about the Keims' place. I know Rosie will be really excited to hear that."

Rosie? "*Jah*. She is."

"As soon as the rest of our harvest is in, I plan to go and help her *vatter* out as much as I can."

"That's *gut*. They will appreciate the help, for sure and certain."

Zach was dying to know how their date went, but it wasn't proper to ask. Maybe if he just beat around the bush a little, John would spill the beans.

"Oh, man, Zach. Rosie is amazing. I know that we've only been out riding once, but I think she's the one for me."

"Really?" How on earth could he know that from a single date?

"Yeah. I think you were wrong about her. She didn't seem stuck on herself at all to me." He took a rag from a hook on the wall and wiped his hands. "Did you know that she wants to go see the Millers' cave with me? I mean, what girl is interested in caves—even after you tell her there are bats inside?"

"So you two hit it off, huh?" He tried his utmost to mask his true feelings.

"I can't wait to see her again. Do you think it would be too forward of me to come calling?"

"Uh, I don't know… I mean with all the people that are there."

"You're right. I guess I'll just have to be patient." He turned back to look at his horse and gave her a gentle pat. "Hey, you doing anything now? Wanna go fishing?"

"Sure." Now, *this* was a topic he was more comfortable discussing. No hiding his emotions. "May I use your extra pole?"

"Of course. I'll just be a minute. I need to let *Mamm* know where I'm going."

Zach watched John disappear into the house, then return a moment later with a paper bag in his hand.

"*Mamm* said to tell you to stay for supper after we get back from fishing." John smiled.

"I'd love to. What's in the bag?"

"Just some snacks." He gestured toward the stream. "Let's go?"

Zachariah nodded. After grabbing the fishing poles and tackle box from the barn, the two of them set off toward the stream that flowed at the bottom of one of the rugged hills on the Christners' property. It was a place they'd frequented over the years. One of the things Zach appreciated about living in Kentucky was the beautiful topography. Hills, streams, and trees aplenty adorned the landscape which created a sense of serenity. Zach thought that if there was a paradise on earth, it might just be Kentucky. There was no place he'd rather be.

"Rosanna! Rosanna, where—Oh, there you are!" Frances approached the tree's low hanging branch where Rosanna sat. "Why are you over here by yourself when all the fun is at the house?"

She eyed her sister warily. "I just feel kind of nervous. There are so many people and I don't really know anyone."

"Well, you know us, silly. And you know Lizzie and Patricia; they just got here. And there's a lot of handsome young men who would most likely want to know you too," Frances added slyly.

John came to Rosanna's mind and she smiled. "Okay, I'll come."

"*Gut*!" Frances started off, then looked back and gestured for Rosanna. "Come on! Let's go!"

Rosanna followed her sister at a more sedate pace and couldn't help but feel her shyness creep over her again as the multitude of unfamiliar Amish folk came into view.

It was the Saturday Bishop Hershberger and her father had decided upon for the frolic and everyone in the community seemed to be here, including John Christner. He'd sent her a smile and a quick wink when he'd first arrived, which warmed her heart. For sure and for certain, John was winning her over.

Lizzie approached her. "Rosanna, I've been looking for you everywhere. How are you?"

"*Wunderbaar*. How are you, Lizzie?"

"*Gut*, especially now that you're here. Do you know if the women are starting on the meal yet?"

She shook her head. "I don't think so. *Mamm* said eleven. We put snacks out earlier."

"Then we have almost an hour! Will you show me around?"

"I'd love to. Come with me." She and Lizzie headed for the forest and Rosanna began explaining, "We have fifty acres altogether, forty-two of which are woods." The girls entered the dense copse of trees on an overgrown path. "As you can probably tell, we'll need some animals to get the grass back down to a reasonable height. My father's considering putting up fences and bringing in animals to start on that while we still live at the Zooks'. Just so a lot of it will be taken care of before we move in. If they eat the foliage, they can drink out of the creek."

Lizzie nodded. "Sounds reasonable. How far is the creek?"

"It's a bit of a walk to get there. It's down yonder. Do you want to see it?"

"Sure. I saw it several years ago, when the Borntregers were still here, but it's been a while." They moved down the path a couple beats before Lizzie spoke again. "How are you liking it here so far?"

"It's nice. The land is beautiful, and everyone I've met so far has been friendly." *Perhaps a little too friendly*, she thought, remembering Zach's forward behavior.

"I'm glad you like it. And I'm glad you came. I'm sure it wasn't easy. Did you leave a lot of friends behind?"

"A few. But I mostly miss Magdalena. She's my closest friend."

"I imagine it's difficult. I don't really have a good friend, other than my sister. And the good thing about being friends with her, is I don't have to worry about either of us moving away until we marry. Otherwise, we're stuck together."

Rosanna smiled.

"Oh, I'd been meaning to ask you, how did your first day of school go? Any trouble from the *kinner*?"

"No, they were good. Atlee Gingrich tried to stir up some mischief the next day, but nothing serious. So far, all is well."

"That's nice to hear. Are you excited about the young folks' gathering tonight?"

"You mean the hoedown?"

"*Jah*. They're always a lot of fun!"

"I'm looking forward to it. I'm not used to hearing music with instruments. Back home that was always frowned upon."

"It's not here. The ministers don't approve of it outright, but they let us do it anyway, so long as we aren't baptized into the church yet. I'm sure you'll love it. One of the boys even plays a guitar!"

"I don't know if I've ever heard one played in person."

"They're really pretty. If ever I was to learn an instrument, it'd be that one."

Rosanna nodded to the landscape up ahead. "Look, there's the creek."

"Wow. It sure looks different from what I remembered, with everything grown over. I don't remember that beaver dam there either."

"*Dat* plans to take that down right away and clear up the stream."

"My *dat* says that beavers are just a plain menace. He doesn't like them a bit."

Rosanna shrugged. "I think they're cute."

"Maybe." Lizzie glanced back at the dam. "Speaking of cute, perhaps we should get back to the house. I like watching the young men work. Somehow, seeing their raw strength and then thinking about how gently they can treat you gives me shivers." She smiled.

"I see. You're a romantic." Rosanna laughed. "Alright. Let's go."

"What has put that smile on your face?" Lizzie sidled up to Rosanna at one of the young folks' gatherings.

"*Ach*, nothing," Rosanna insisted. She glanced discreetly at John, who'd been watching her from across the room as he played his harmonica. She loved the twinkle in his eye that evidenced there was a smile behind his instrument.

Lizzie noticed and peeked his way as well, before meeting Rosanna's gaze with a grin. "Uh-huh. Word from the rumor mill says you've been riding home with John Christner an awful lot."

Rosanna subdued a smile. "I have. What about it?"

"How's it going with you two?"

"It's been nice."

Lizzie raised a brow. "Nice? That's it? That's all you can say? I've known John my entire life and I'd say he's a lot more than just nice."

"What do you mean by that?"

"John is one of the sweetest people I've ever known. When I was nine, I'd forgotten to bring my lunch to school one day. John had apparently noticed and pretended he didn't like peanut butter and jelly sandwiches that day; he asked me to eat it for him.

"If someone wasn't having a good day, he'd go and tell them jokes until they laughed and forgot all about what made them sad.

"Another time, he asked Martha Yoder to ride home with him from a singing."

She frowned. "I don't understand."

"You maybe haven't met Martha yet. She's the one with Down syndrome. She only comes because she likes to sing and she always rides home with her brother."

"That's very kind. I already knew he was a sweetheart. How come he doesn't have an *aldi* already?" Rosanna wondered aloud.

Lizzie shrugged. "I suppose he's just never found a girl that's right for him, though there are plenty of girls who've had their eye on him at some point in time."

Rosanna sent her a questioning glance.

Lizzie laughed. "Not me. He's handsome enough, and I'd be foolish not to consider him, but he's just a friend to me. Besides, I've got David Mast." She nodded toward the table with the snacks. "See the one with the blond hair by the drinks?"

"With the blue or green shirt?"

"Green. That's David. The one in blue is his brother, Danny."

The young man glanced up and caught them looking. His face flushed a brilliant hue and he held Lizzie's gaze for a second before turning back to his conversation.

Lizzie grinned. "He turns red as a tomato all the time. I think it's the most adorable thing."

"How long have you been courting?"

"Almost two months. Can you believe he had his brother ask me to ride home in his buggy for him?"

"Isn't that how they do it here?"

"Not usually." She shrugged. "If a boy likes you, he usually just comes and asks directly."

"It's interesting how different it is here, compared to how it was back home." She sipped some of her tea. "He must be incredibly shy."

"He is. I don't mind though." Lizzie smiled at something past Rosanna. "Well, I better go get myself something to drink."

"Okay." Curious as to why she was leaving so abruptly, Rosanna turned to see John standing a few feet behind her. "Oh, hi."

"You sound disappointed." He frowned.

She smiled. "No, I'm definitely not. I was just surprised to see you there."

"Well, *gut*. For a second there, I thought you were expecting some other handsome young Amish man to be waiting for you and my heart would be utterly shattered." He pressed a hand to his heart dramatically.

She shook her head. "No need for shattered hearts. I promised to ride home with *you* and I intend to."

They made their move to the exit. "I hope you're riding home with me out of more than just duty."

Her eyes met his. "I am."

John opened the door and grinned. He gallantly crooked his arm at his side, once they were outside away from the crowd. "M'lady."

She obliged with a smile, gently grasping his arm as he escorted her to his buggy.

Chapter Five

The school week was finally over and Rosanna had bidden farewell to the last student just a few moments ago. She usually walked home with the Zook girls, but she wanted to stay and read through some of the week's assignments she'd given to the children. While the scholars' work ended on Friday at school, her work continued over the weekend until the week's grading was completed and the assignments for the following week were prepared. It would be much easier to tackle those tasks in the quiet of an empty schoolhouse than it would be in the Zooks' busy household.

Churning of buggy wheels on gravel outside caused Rosanna to glance up at the clock. Oh good, it was only four o'clock. She thought that maybe she'd stayed too long and someone from the Zook household had come to bring her home. Who could be here?

She stood up from the desk just as the main door to the schoolhouse opened.

"I hope you don't mind me showing up here."

"John?" Now, *he* was the last person she expected to see. "What are you doing here?"

"I figured you might still be working, so I decided to swing by." He frowned. "You don't mind, do ya?"

"Uh, no. Of course, not."

"Could you use a ride home?"

She grimaced. "I'm not quite finished with my work. I had just planned on walking back home."

"I can take you, and I'll wait if you'd like," he offered. "And if you're hungry, we can go into town and get something to eat. Or a milkshake or something."

"Well, that does sound *gut* but I still have some grading to do." She glanced back at the remaining stack of assignments and weighed her options. Did she really want to miss out on spending time with this handsome young man? "I guess I can finish them tomorrow at home."

"You can do them now if you need to. I really don't mind waiting."

"*Nee*, it's okay."

"So, you'll come with me then?" She didn't miss the excitement in his voice.

"*Jah.*"

"*Wunderbaar!*"

She began gathering the things on her desk.

"Here, I can help with that." He put both his arms out in front of him and waited for her to load them up with her homework.

Rosanna carried her purse and locked the door behind them, after making sure she'd turned off the last lamp. She followed John to his buggy and hopped up into it. It looked a little different during daylight hours.

It seemed like anytime they'd gone anywhere it had been at night. Now that there was sufficient light, she could see that he'd made an extra effort to make his courting buggy special. She'd already known about the radio because they'd listened to it a few times before, but now she could see that the wood on the dashboard had been lacquered and possibly stained. The seat cushion was extra thick and had been covered in a luxurious hunter green velvet-like material. Rosanna almost felt like a queen riding in an expensive carriage.

"Your buggy is very nice." She rubbed her hands on the seat cushion enjoying its softness.

"Do you like it? I designed it myself."

"I do." She briefly wondered how many *maed* had ridden in the very spot she was now sitting in and it stole a bit of her joy. Just how many girls *had* John courted?

"Something wrong?"

"No, it's nothing."

"Rosie, whatever you have to say, you can say it. I wanna know what you're thinking."

She hesitated and blew out a breath. "I was just wondering how many other *maed* have been in this same seat."

He shrugged, eyeing her cautiously. "A few."

"Oh."

"But none of them ever captured my heart like you have." He reached over and grasped her hand.

"You, Mr. Christner, happen to be a charmer of the worst kind." She pulled her hand away.

He looked up at the sky. "I pay her a compliment and she accuses me of being insincere. How much can one heart take?" He placed both hands over his heart. "Oh, the agony."

Rosanna laughed.

"And she laughs at my calamity!"

She shook her head. "How on earth do you keep a straight face?"

"I'm dying inside."

"Really?"

"No. I've spent countless hours in front of the mirror telling jokes to myself and forcing myself not to laugh."

"Really?"

"No. Well, actually, that's partially true. I have done it once or twice."

"So, being completely serious, why did you come by today?"

"I thought that was clear. You have undoubtedly captured my heart. It is bound with chains and I don't know if I'll ever be able to break free."

"That was supposed to be serious?" She laughed.

"Well, I'd kiss you to prove it but I'm afraid of retaliation."

"Retaliation?"

"Yeah, you know, like a shoe or purse aimed at my face."

Her smile widened. "And you're not willing to risk it?"

"Wow, was that just an invitation to kiss you? Because that's what it sounded like to me."

"I suppose at some point in time I might let you kiss me."

"Would that some point in time happen to be today?"

She smiled. "We'll have to see about that."

"Well, until then, I will just have to bear the sting of unrequited love."

Rosanna began laughing so hard, her stomach protested with pain. It took her a full three minutes of huffing and puffing to regain her composure.

"And I didn't even intend for that to be funny." John smiled.

Rosanna lifted a hand. "Don't get me started again."

He made a zipping motion over his mouth, but held in a chuckle.

"Okay. Pull this buggy over," she insisted.

"Out here? In the middle of nowhere?"

"Yes."

He shrugged. "As you wish." He pulled the buggy to the side of the road and set the brake. "Okay, now what?"

"Close your eyes."

"What?"

"Just close them." She put a hand on her hip.

He finally did as bidden. "I don't know if I like where this is headed."

Rosanna waved a hand in front of his eyes to be sure he wasn't peeking. "You're not peeking, are you?"

"Is that against the rules?"

"Yes, it's against the rules." Her exasperation was evident in her tone.

"Okay, fine. I'm not peeking."

"Promise?"

He squeezed his eyes shut and nodded.

For the life of him, John couldn't figure out what on earth Rosanna was up to. He was dying to sneak a gander, but he'd promised he wouldn't. And if he had any chance of a future with this beautiful girl who laughed at all his silly jokes, he'd better keep his promises.

They sat there in silence for what seemed like an eternity until...

Whoa! Warm, soft lips touched his and sent a thrill up his spine. He opened his eyes for a fraction of a second to make sure it was real. He wasn't dreaming, it was very real. He gladly pulled Rosanna closer and returned her sweet kiss which ended all too soon.

He opened his eyes. "That was the nicest thing anyone's done for me in a long time. Can we do that again?"

Rosanna bit her lip. Was she self-conscious about her forward behavior?

He didn't wait for an audible answer. Her eyes told him all he needed to know. She wanted more.

This time, he leaned forward and met her lips. Her warm hands wrapped around his back and neck, pulling him even closer. He was afraid that if he stopped, this lovely dream would come to an end. A groan of pleasure from somewhere deep within escaped his lips unbidden.

"Rosanna..." His heart quickened in his chest and he knew they really should stop. *Now.* He forced himself away. "Whew! I don't think I've ever experienced that kind of kissing before. Girl, you know what you're doing."

Her eyelids lowered and her cheeks blossomed with color. "I do?"

He shook his head. "Oh my, do you ever!"

The sound of clip clop from another buggy was approaching, but he couldn't see it just yet.

"We'd better go now, *jah*?"

"Yes, we'd better." He released the brake and signaled to the horse, and with a light flick of the reins, they were on their way. Their quite wonderful, glorious way to a promising future.

John sighed in contentment. *She kissed me!*

Zachariah heard the turn of buggy wheels entering the driveway and knew it had to be Rosanna returning home. He'd gone by the schoolhouse earlier to see if she'd needed a ride but she hadn't been there. Now he knew why. John had picked her up.

The window from his second-story room gave him a bird's-eye view. He really shouldn't be watching his best friend like this, but he couldn't seem to help himself. When the buggy reached the hitching post and John got out, Zach descended the stairs to greet his friend.

Rosanna entered the kitchen through the back door and was smiling until her eyes met his. She quickly looked away and moved past him, making a beeline for her room. He groaned inwardly out of frustration. Could she not even acknowledge him? It had been months since he tried to kiss her.

As he opened the door to step outside, he heard his mother's voice.

He turned back. "Yeah, *Mamm*?"

"Be sure to ask John to stay for supper. It's just about ready."

"Okay, *Mamm*," he called back as he headed out the door for the second time.

His friend greeted him. "Oh, good. I was hoping

you'd come out and say hello. I need to talk to you about something important."

Zachariah frowned and nodded. "Before you do, I have a message from my mother. She said to ask you to stay for supper."

"Ah, man, I'd love to but I really need to get back home. I told *Daed* I wouldn't be gone long and I've already been out too long." He frowned. "Hey, would you come by tonight?"

"Sure."

"I'll save you some dessert."

"I'll definitely be there." Zach smiled.

"I knew you'd take a bribe."

"Hey, bribe or no, I always have time for you."

John cupped his shoulder. "That's good to know, friend." He went to unhitch his horse. "I better git. See you in a while."

"I'll be there."

Chapter Six

Rosanna sat on the porch swing contemplating the events of the day, which seemed to have become a nightly ritual. She couldn't seem to get her mind off John since he'd dropped her off that afternoon. Their trip into town proved to be rather uneventful, other than their brief roadside distraction. She surprised herself today—something that didn't happen often. She still couldn't believe her forwardness, but with John Christner, the kiss just seemed so natural.

He said she'd stolen his heart, but she certainly wasn't the only thief in this equation. No, they were partners in crime. She smiled, thinking of how John might respond to her conclusions. John had everything a girl could want; he was kind, considerate, funny, and quite handsome in her eyes. How could she resist falling in love with a guy like that? Yep, it seemed like John Christner would most likely become her life mate. And, oh, how wonderful that would be! Was it possible to know that after courting only three months?

She wondered where Zachariah had disappeared to after supper until his mother mentioned something about him visiting John. She didn't desire to separate the two friends, but she also didn't want either one of them to kiss and tell. Not that she'd kissed Zach. But if Zach told John that he'd kissed her, she wondered how John would react.

"Hey." Zach's voice caught her off guard.

"Hey."

"Do you mind if we talk a little bit?"

"I don't know, John might—"

"I'll sit over here. I promise not to come too close. Contrary to popular belief, I can control myself." He took a seat in one of the old hickory rockers his folks had probably owned forever, by the look of them. It was amazing the antiques still held up.

"Okay, I guess that would be fine." She eyed the large manila envelope he held. "What's in there?"

He shrugged. "Just some stuff." He ran a hand through his hair. "I just came from John's. He's pretty captivated by you."

She lifted a small smile.

"I'm guessing the feeling is mutual?"

She began to nod and then stopped. "Where are you going with this conversation?"

"I just need to figure some things out, that's all." He lightly tapped the envelope between his hands.

"Like?"

"Never mind. Just, if you're going to lead John on, then don't drop him."

"What kind of a girl do you think I am? I'm not playing any games."

"Good. Just, don't."

He got up from the rocker and looked straight at her. Was that turmoil in his eyes? He looked down at his hands. Did he want to say something more? He appeared to be holding back.

"Goodbye, Rosanna." He walked into the house and closed the door behind him.

Zachariah tossed and turned all night long, unable to sleep more than a few minutes. He hadn't been prepared for John's sudden news at all. Was his friend already that serious about his newfound love? Apparently so, and the feeling was mutual.

There was only one thing to do and it would probably be the most difficult choice he'd ever have to make. In a way, it was the easy way out. Not that it would be easy at all. Far from it. But at least he wouldn't have to see his best friend and the girl of his dreams falling more in love with each other, day in and day out. He decided to do what a real friend should do—he needed to step out of the way. And if he was going to do that, he had to leave.

It would be a sacrifice for sure and certain.

A shrill cry pierced Rosanna's ears and woke her from a dead sleep. She'd been having such a lovely dream, but she could no longer think about that. Something was wrong. Something must be terribly wrong.

She and her sisters, who had also awakened, quickly

dressed and flew to where the commotion had been heard. She never would have anticipated the scene before her. Elnora and Abram Zook sat on the living room couch in tears. Elnora clutched a letter to her chest and rocked back and forth. The Zook children—everyone but Zachariah—stood around crying as well. Had someone died? Where on earth was Zach?

She looked to her mother, who attempted to comfort Elnora. "*Was is letz?*"

Elnora looked up with tears cascading down her face. "Zachariah has left. He…he's becoming a soldier!"

A soldier? "What? Why?" Rosanna frowned.

"We don't know. He's never said anything about joining the military," Zach's father said shaking his head.

"He'd always seemed so happy here." At least, he seemed to be until Rosanna had turned him down. Her heart sank. Had she been the reason he left?

Something didn't add up. Was he really joining the military or did he just say he was to prevent his family from looking for him?

"He never spoke of leaving. He loves the ways of our people. I don't understand this. Why would he bring this shame upon his family?" His father choked out the words. "We will pray to *Der Herr* to bring him back. *Der Herr* will bring him back." He began sobbing.

Rosanna didn't know what to do. How could she comfort this family who now grieved over their son? Zachariah leaving and becoming a soldier was like turning his back on everything he'd ever been taught and embracing a life that was polar opposite to what his family held sacred. How could he take up arms against another human being, if that was, in fact, what he was doing? This was not the Amish way.

Losing a child to the world was one of the worst things an Amish family could endure. It was akin to a death in the family. But knowing that Zachariah had joined the military was like an extra blow. Surely, at death, his remains would be buried outside of the cemetery in an unmarked grave. That was where those who died without the Amish church were buried. Undoubtedly, he'd be condemned to Hell. It was a scourge that couldn't be forgotten quickly enough.

Anger rose in Rosanna's throat. How could Zach do this to those who'd always cared for him and provided for all his needs? How could he do this to the ones who loved him the most? And what about his best friend? Surely John would be grieved over his friend's departure. If Zachariah were here, she'd surely give him a piece of her mind. Pure selfishness, that's what it was. Never in her life had she ever met a more egotistical person.

A thought now occurred to her. What if she could find Zach and talk some sense into him? Where had he gone? She didn't know much about the military, but didn't they have a place where the soldiers stayed? How would she get that type of information? Perhaps she could find the *Englisch* driver that no doubt took him to wherever Zachariah had told them to. *Jah*, that is what she would do and she'd enlist John to help.

Chapter Seven

Rosanna didn't know whether she should go over to John's place to let him know what had happened or wait until the singing tomorrow night. She didn't think she'd be able to stand waiting that long. Besides, the longer she waited, the more difficult it would be to find Zachariah. Surely, John would want to know as soon as possible. If it was Rosanna's best friend who'd left, she'd want to know right away, no matter how difficult the news would be.

One problem existed though. Where did John live? She'd never been to his house before, so she really had no clue. Should she ask one of Zach's brothers? Apparently, she'd have to ask someone if she had any hope of finding the place.

A half hour later, Rosanna's hand was poised to knock on the door of the Christner home. She briefly deliberated whether this was a good idea or not. Would John's family think she'd come over to share a tidbit of gossip just to see him? She tossed her silly thoughts aside. With bated breath, she knocked twice in quick succession.

"Rosie?"

Rosanna forced a half-smile. "Can we talk?"

His sympathetic look revealed his concern. "Sure." He glanced behind him. "Let's go for walk."

With jacket in hand, John joined her outside. "Is everything okay?"

"It's Zachariah. He's gone." She couldn't help the fresh tears after remembering his folks' deep anguish.

He pulled her close and held her tight.

She felt a little foolish crying like this since she hadn't even known Zach that well. Not like John, who was his best friend and had known him his entire life. "He's become a soldier."

Why had John's body stiffened? Most likely because the Amish were so against fighting, Rosanna answered her unspoken question. She stepped back and looked into his eyes. He wore an expression she couldn't read. How in the world was he being so calm about all this?

He sighed. "We will miss him."

"I had an idea. What if we went to look for him? We could talk some sense into him and bring him back."

John held up a hand and shook his head. "I don't know if that's such a good idea."

"But he's your best friend. Don't you even want him to come back home?"

"It's not that, Rosie. If Zach left, I'm sure he had his reasons. And if I know Zach, he'll come back to us."

"How can you be sure?" She'd known others who'd left and said they were coming back but they never did.

The world seemed to hold too much appeal for former Amish seeking something different. It was as though the devil took hold of them and wouldn't let go.

John sighed. "He said he would."

She studied him. "You…you knew?"

"We talked about it yesterday when he came over. Don't worry, he's not going away forever."

"How long will he be gone?"

"Two years, most likely."

"*Two years*? But he—" Rosanna frowned. She wouldn't burden John with her fears for his best friend. How could he still think Zach would come back after being out in the world for two years? In her mind, the chances of Zach's return were miniscule. "I don't think he'll return."

"Well, it's Zach's life. If he chooses to stay *Englisch*, that will be *his* choice."

"You're losing your best friend."

He shook his head. "I don't see it that way. Zach's friendship goes a lot deeper than that. Amish or no, I won't hold it against him."

Did he have any idea what he was saying? If Zach stayed *Englisch* that meant the pull would be that much stronger for John. She couldn't bear to lose both of them.

Rosanna couldn't help the tears that welled in her eyes again. "You don't plan to leave too, do you?"

John held her at arm's length and gazed into her eyes. "And leave the girl of my dreams? Not a chance. There's no way on this earth I'd leave you, Rosie, so lay your fears to rest." He brushed her cheek with his thumb.

John pulled her close and caressed her lips with his.

"Rosie, I have every intention of growing old with you. I can't picture anybody else by my side."

"How can you know so soon? We haven't even known each other very long."

"It's been long enough. Rosie, every time I'm with you, something inside me confirms it. From the first time I took you home from the singing, I've known. We won't get married till next year at the soonest, but in my mind I don't see why we should wait long." He grasped her hand. "Of course, I want you to be sure it's what you want as well."

"I am fond of you, John, and I do care for you. A lot. But I will definitely need time."

"I'd wait for you as long as I have to, but if it's more than a decade…" he shook his head.

Rosanna giggled. "A decade?"

"I'm trying to mentally prepare myself for the worst." He smiled. "See, that's why I know you're the one. Nobody laughs at my silly jokes like you do. And laughter can overcome anything. You get mad at me, I just tell you a joke."

Rosanna laughed again.

"See? Yep, you're *definitely* the one." He drew her near again and kissed the top of her head.

Chapter Eight

Noticing the time, Rosanna tapped her small bell three times to signal the beginning of recess. The quiet room instantly became alive with conversation and laughter as her students swarmed the exit. She watched the children make their escape before getting to her feet and crisscrossing through the desks to the window. Her view was the left side of the schoolyard, where various games were being played. Remembering how she and Magdalena would chase each other nearly every break brought a smile to her lips. She returned to her desk and back to the essay she'd been grading. Zach's sister Julia had written it.

She sighed. Julia's schoolwork had been lacking considerably since her brother's departure. Rosanna wished she knew how to help her.

Raised voices met her ears and she leapt up. Pausing to glance out the window, she spotted Julia and Loretta standing side by side, facing several of the other students. She hurried outside.

"My *vatter* says your brother is damned to Hell! He's left his Amish roots and ain't never gonna return!" Silas Troyer sneered.

"He's probably out there shooting people right now! He's a murderer. And we all know murderers don't go to Heaven."

"Does that mean you're gonna leave too? Are you gonna join your brother and go to Hell?"

Rosanna was fuming by the time she realized what the ruckus was about. "Children, stop this right now!"

The scholars turned at her sharp tone.

"I am terribly ashamed of all of you, acting like this! *Gott* says to love one another, not to condemn. Why would good, Amish *kinner* turn on their own and disobey God? Think about that. I want every one of you to write an essay on compassion. I'll expect it tomorrow! You may all head back to class."

The children shuffled toward the schoolhouse.

"Silas Troyer, Mose Mast, and Atlee Gingrich, you three stay here!" Rosanna waited until she had the instigators' attention. "If I ever hear any of you talking like that to Julia or Loretta or anyone else again, you can be certain there will be consequences! I will be speaking to each of your parents about this."

Silas opened his mouth.

She held up a hand, still seething. "I don't want to hear a single word from you, Silas Troyer! Now all three of you go inside."

They swiftly obeyed.

Her anger subsided as she turned to find Julia and Loretta standing where they had been attacked. Julia hugged her younger sister, who was crying on her shoulder. Tears sprung to her own eyes as she stepped toward them and held them both. "I'm so sorry," she whispered.

"It's okay, Teacher. It wasn't your fault." Julia seemed to be attempting nonchalance, though moisture glimmered in her eyes.

Rosanna couldn't help but pin the fault squarely on the shoulders of whom it belonged—Zachariah Zook.

"How could he just leave them like that? Does he even have any idea of what he's doing to them?" Rosanna threw her hands into the air.

John frowned. "I can't believe those boys would be so cruel."

"That's not what I'm talking about, John! It's not the boys' fault. I mean, it is their fault for being unkind but they shouldn't have had the opportunity. This is all Zach's fault. When he left, it was like he put a big target on the backs of his family members and opened them up to heartache and vulnerability of the worst kind. How could he do that? I don't understand it. Did he not even consider the consequences?"

"Maybe he just felt he had to get away. Maybe he felt trapped and wanted to try something new, to do something different. I'm sure he didn't mean for all this to happen, Rosie. He couldn't have known his sisters would be bullied."

His total lack of emotion astounded her. "How would they not be? And how are you so calm about this? I mean, even though you had warning and you already knew he was going to jump the fence, you don't even seem…angry, hurt, confused, upset. I am, and I didn't even know Zach well. How can you be so calm about this? You almost seem like you…agree with him."

John pulled the buggy off to the side of the road. "Listen, Rosie." He sighed. "Zach… I guess I just… understand him. If I didn't have someone special, if I didn't have you, I could see why he would do something so drastic. Sometimes, you feel like your life is just stuck in place. It seems like nothing you do is of any importance and everything is just, I don't know, paused, maybe? Like you're stuck inside a clock that stopped working. And when you feel like that, you'll try anything to feel different, to feel significant again."

"Wow. I never—Did *you* feel like that?"

He nodded. "But that was before I met you. Then everything changed." He smiled and ran a finger down her nose.

She couldn't resist a small smile. "I still can't understand. And I don't think what Zach did was right."

"Let's not talk about Zach anymore. We should be having fun." He turned to her. "I spoke with Gideon Miller and he said we can go explore their cave any time we want."

"Really?"

"Mm-hm. So I'm thinking, you and me could go on Saturday and have a picnic?" He wiggled his eyebrows. "What do you say?"

"I'd love to go!"

"Good. Saturday, it is." John grasped the reins and urged the horse back onto the road.

"And it's 'you and I'." She playfully poked his ribs.

"What?"

"You said 'you and me could go on Saturday,' but the correct term would be 'you and I.'"

John shook his head, grinning. "That's the problem with you school teachers. You can't never have no fun."

"You can't ever have any fun." She shoved his shoulder. "That's not true. We just prefer to be correct while having fun."

"Mm-hm." He sent her a dubious expression and she laughed.

Chapter Nine

Never in a million years would Zach have imagined he'd be walking in a desert on the other side of the globe—toting a machine gun, no less. He could hardly believe this was his reality. His mind fought against itself daily as he battled the right and wrong in regard to war. He'd been taught all his life to turn the other cheek, to love your enemies, and that it was wrong to kill another human being, yet now he *had to* believe it was…okay?

What had he gotten himself into?

When he looked into the mirror, he barely recognized himself. He'd never had short hair before entering the military; it had never been allowed. He admitted that he did like his crew cut, though. But the church leaders would never approve of it.

He mentally rehearsed the orders his platoon had been given. Their job here was to secure the city, but in order to do that they'd need to befriend the local civilians and gain their confidence. They were not the enemy. They were there to protect the townsfolk from the insurgents. Radicals had come in and nearly demolished everything, taking what plunder they could. If the soldiers could derive information from the citizens, they'd be able to locate the insurgents and destroy them. Nobody liked war, but sometimes it was necessary to protect the innocent and to bring peace to a war-torn region.

Basic training hadn't been as difficult as he believed it would be. He chalked that up to his Amish heritage. He'd already been used to getting up early in the morning to tend to the chores before breakfast. They were never allowed to use too much water for showers because their water supply had been limited to the rainfall that filled their cistern before *Dat* added the well, so showers were always short. Growing up, he'd always made his bed without being told to. He knew how to follow orders well and seldom protested when told to do something.

The most difficult for him had been enduring the filthy language and lifestyles of the others. They constantly referred to things he knew nothing about, so he often felt like an outsider. But by the sound of what they described, he was glad he'd been sheltered from those things. It was the height of worldliness, no doubt, and if anyone from back home were there to witness it, he'd be ashamed for sure and certain. But he could put up with it for as long as he had to.

Home back on the farm never sounded so good.

Today was the day! John had thought about it long and hard and decided that this would be the best day to ask her—to ask Rosie to marry him.

He flicked a rein over his horse's back and glanced at his girl sitting beside him.

"I'm so excited to finally see the cave! I'm sure it's beautiful!"

He glanced at her. "It is. But it's not as beautiful as you."

She laughed and pushed his shoulder. "There you go charming again."

"Is there something wrong with complimenting my girl?"

"I suppose not."

"See? And besides, I'm not saying anything that isn't true." He smiled and took her hand in his.

She returned his grin, then gasped. "Oh no! I forgot my flashlight!"

"Don't worry. We can share mine. It's right here." He felt around under the buggy seat. "Shoot! I forgot mine too!"

Her eyes widened. "Seriously?"

He grinned and shook his head, pulling his flashlight out from under the seat. "I'm joshin' ya."

She leveled a mock glare at him before she released a burst of laughter. "I thought we'd have to go back and get one."

"Nah. Even if we didn't bring any, we could just borrow one from the Millers."

"I don't know if I've really met any of the Millers, other than a few of the children. Elizabeth, Mark, and Reuben attend school."

John nodded. "They're the youngest of eleven. Only five are still at home."

"Whoa. That's a lot of *kinner*."

"Not really. My *daed* was one of sixteen."

"Really? I didn't know that."

"Would you not like to have a lot of children?"

Rosie shrugged. "I don't know. I haven't really thought about it much. It was just me and my two sisters so I'm not used to a full house." She paused. "I suppose I would like a large family. Not too big though. I couldn't imagine having sixteen children." She laughed.

"I'm sure having a lot of *kinner* can make things crazy, but the more children you have, the more help you have. They're definitely a blessing."

"I agree. How many *kinner* do you see yourself having?"

He shrugged. "As many as God allows. I won't mind if He gives me one or one hundred."

She smiled. "Well, I doubt He'll be giving you a hundred."

"Me too. Maybe a hundred grandchildren."

"Don't put the cart before the horse now. Grandchildren are a long way off."

"Well, time flies when you're having fun and I intend on having as much fun as I can. Grandchildren will come before we—before *I* know it." John looked to see if Rosie noticed his slip of the tongue. If she did, she didn't show it. Was that a good thing or a bad thing?

They reached the Millers' property before he could decide and pulled up to the hitching post. John helped Rosanna down from the buggy to meet Deacon Miller, who came out to greet them. They chatted for a few moments before John asked about the cave.

"Never seen a cave, have you? Ours is a fine one, if I do say so myself. Make sure you don't disturb the bats though. I'll have Mark take you." Deacon Miller called for his son, who arrived in two shakes of a stick, with a flashlight in hand.

"Howdy, Teacher." The boy smiled at Rosanna.

"Hello, Mark. Are you going to take me to see your cave?"

"Sure am. Follow me." The boy started off and John and Rosanna followed.

"Aaron and Gabe, two of my big brothers, once found some arrowheads in the cave. Probably from the Indians. Who knows how old they could've been. Wouldn't it be neat to discover they were there before Columbus came? I've searched and searched to find more, but I ain't never—" Mark glanced back at Rosanna. "*Haven't ever* seen one."

John grinned, noticing how the boy corrected his grammar for his teacher.

"Some *Englischers* even came once and tried to buy the cave, but *Daed* wouldn't let them. They did take a bunch of pictures of it though. Don't know what for." The boy continued on as the cave came into view. "Here we are. If you want, I can go in with you. I don't have to, though. I've been in there hundreds of times."

Rosanna opened her mouth to speak.

"No, thank you, Mark. We'll be fine." John spoke up before she could say a word, just in case she had any ideas of letting the boy join them.

"Alright, then. Have fun. And watch out for the bats."

Mark turned and ran back to the house, taking his flashlight with him.

Rosie gave John a little shove, feigning exasperation. "Why'd you do that? You didn't let me speak."

"Couldn't chance you inviting the boy along with us, could I?" He grinned. "Besides, what if I want to steal a kiss?"

"I was going to ask him for his flashlight before sending him home," she said, arching a brow.

"Oh." He frowned. "Well, I guess that *would have* been a good idea."

Rosanna sighed dramatically. "Now I'll just have to share with you."

"Would that be so bad?"

"Definitely." Her face was a wall of seriousness and, for a second, he wondered if she really might be upset with him. Then she smirked and John knew he'd been had.

He shook his head. "Come on, troublemaker. Let's go explore."

Rosanna glanced around, then stopped in her tracks. "What should I do with the picnic basket?"

"Well, it'll slow us down if we bring it with us. Why don't we—" John surveyed the area. "I know. Give it here." He reached for the basket and placed it up in a nearby tree. "It should be fine there."

"So long as we don't forget it. My *mamm* wouldn't like for us to lose her basket."

"Oh, I won't forget. The food's inside." He winked. "*Now*, let's explore."

John reached for her hand and walked to the cave's entrance. "Careful here. It goes down a little ways."

Rosanna followed him as he lit the way with his flashlight. "Wow. It's really dark in here."

"Yep. Just wait until we go a little further. Then all we'll have is the flashlight." He measured his pace, so as not to move too fast for Rosie.

"It has plenty of battery left, right?"

"Yeah. It'll be fine."

John picked his way down the incline and reached the bottom. Rosie bumped into him from behind.

"Sorry. I didn't see you."

"I don't mind. You can hold on to me if you want."

Her warm hands found his arm and clung to it. John decided a woman holding on to him was the best feeling he'd ever experienced. It gave him a sense of leadership and significance. He enjoyed being the strong one, the protector. Maybe they should explore dark places more often. Or, maybe not—at least not until they were married.

"There's just this one room but it's quite large." He shined his flashlight throughout the cave as they wandered around.

"Oh, my!" She followed the beam of his flashlight. "It's beautiful! And look at the stalactite and stalagmite formations!"

"I always forget which one grows from the ground and which one's from the ceiling."

"Just remember, stalactites with a 'c' are on the ceiling, while stalagmites with a 'g' are on the ground. Once I learned that, I never got them confused."

"That's smart. I never thought of that."

"Associations help stimulate the mind. Things tend to be easier to remember if you can relate them to something else."

"Hmm… I see. Like the notes in music—Every Good Boy Does Fine and All Cows Eat Grass."

"That's right!"

"You enjoy teaching, don't you?"

She nodded and smiled.

John directed the beam of light at an area of the ceiling where he knew there would be bats. "See those?"

"What are they?"

"Bats."

"Oh. So many?" Her volume dropped. "Stop shining the light on them. They might wake up!" she whispered.

He laughed. "They aren't likely to wake up unless you throw something at them or are really loud. They're pretty sound sleepers."

"They may sleep well, but there's nothing pretty about them. Quit shining the light on them."

He kept it on the animals for another couple seconds just to frustrate her.

She shook her head. "Give me the flashlight."

He obeyed and she stepped away, no longer touching him at all. John swallowed his disappointment.

"Look! There's a little tunnel in the wall over there." She headed toward it and he followed. "Are you sure there's only one room?"

He nodded. "They explored the tunnel but it only goes a few dozen feet before it gets too small to fit through."

She surveyed the outlet with the flashlight. "You can't tell by looking at it."

"Do you want to crawl through and see for yourself?"

"No. I don't want to get my dress too dirty, or run into any creatures or anything." She shivered. "You know, it's pretty cold in here."

"That's just 'cuz you aren't holding on to me anymore," he teased.

"You may be right." She slipped her hand in his and smiled.

They wandered around, exploring nooks and crannies, stalactites and stalagmites, until Rosanna's curiosity was at last appeased. John did his best to act as he always did and hide his anticipation. He wanted to propose during or after their picnic lunch, so he was eager to get to it and hopefully put an end to his nervousness.

Rosie laid their picnic blanket out beside the cave entrance and settled onto it, basket in hand. John plopped down beside her. "What'd you bring?"

"I brought fried chicken, macaroni 'n' cheese, and some watermelon."

"Sounds delicious." He watched her as she unpacked two paper plates.

"It probably isn't warm anymore, but hopefully it'll taste all right."

"I'm sure it will." He smiled.

She finished bringing out their meal and they bowed their heads in silent prayer for a moment. They settled into a comfortable quiet.

"How have your students been? Have there been any more issues with Zach's sisters?"

She frowned. "Yes and no. There haven't been any more outbursts like the one before but I know there's definitely tension. Julia and Loretta are always by themselves. They don't play with the other children anymore and I don't think the *kinner* would let them even if they wanted to. I wish I could change it, but I can't *make* the other students accept them. It's worse for Loretta than Julia, I think. Julia will finish her school next year, but Loretta still has another two grades."

Perhaps he shouldn't have brought it up. "You can't make them change. All you can do is be the best example that you can."

She sighed. "I know. I just wish it was different."

John wasn't sure of what to say, so he kept silent and ate his lunch. "This fried chicken is yummy."

She smiled. "Not delicious?"

"It's both. It's yummilicious."

Rosie smiled and shook her head.

"What? It's a good word. Makes perfect sense." He grinned. "Does the teacher not approve of my made-up word?"

"No. The teacher loves your new word!"

"Well, that's good. I aim to please." He took another piece of fried chicken and held it up, slowly taking a bite as though savoring each flavor. Rosanna's giggles informed him of his success. He'd much rather see her happy than distraught over her scholars. "Did you make it?"

"What? The chicken?"

He nodded, enjoying another piece.

She shook her head. "My mother. I haven't mastered the art of fried chicken yet. I did make the mac 'n' cheese though."

"Well, it is also yummilicious." He winked.

She smiled. "You like making people laugh, don't you?"

He nodded and leaned closer. "Especially you." His gaze dropped to her lips as he neared her.

Rosie laughed and handed him a napkin. "You better wipe your mouth first if you plan on kissing me. You've got chicken grease all over yourself."

John accepted the napkin and wiped his mouth clean, grinning. "I thought I was the one with the sense of humor. There. Am I oil-free now?"

She eyed his lips. "Well…" She reached toward him and swiped at the corner of his mouth. "Now you're good."

He took a drink of his water. "So now you'll let me kiss you?"

She nodded and leaned forward, shutting her eyes with a smile.

As tempted as he was to simply gaze upon her pretty face, his desire overpowered that temptation and he met her lips with his in a gentle yet passionate kiss. Drawing her form closer to him, he realized once again that this was the woman he longed to spend the rest of his life with.

"I want to marry you," he murmured.

Rosanna's lips left his and her pretty eyelashes opened to reveal wide eyes. "You do?"

He nodded, absently rubbing her arm. "I do. As soon as we can. In the next wedding season."

"Are—Are you asking—?"

"You to marry me? Yes. Definitely. I am." He nodded again. "Will you marry me, Rosie? Please?"

Her mouth parted, most likely in surprise, and he kept going.

"I love you, Rosie. So very much. And I want to marry you. I know we would be wonderful together. You laugh at my silly jokes and you are so beautiful. And you can kiss—Goodness, you can kiss! And you are so sweet and kind to me, to your students, to everyone. You make me feel so alive and blessed. I know I don't deserve you. And I—" He stopped when her lips met his. Her fingers wove into his hair and sent desire spiraling through his veins. His arms moved of their own accord and pulled her nearer until she was closer to him than anyone had ever been.

When they finally separated, they were both breathless. "I'm guessing that was a yes?"

Rosie nodded, then grinned, and threw her arms around his neck and laughed. John wished he were standing so he could twirl her in his arms. She pulled back and held his face in her hands. "I love you, John Christner. And I would love to marry you." She kissed him again, briefly, then laughed. "I don't know if I've ever been so happy!"

He wrapped his arms around her in an embrace. "I hope that never changes."

Rosanna couldn't wipe the silly grin off her face as she sat down at her desk to write a letter to her best friend.

Dear Magdalena,
Greetings in the name of our Lord!
I am so excited! I wonder if you'll be able to

feel it when you read these words. You'll never guess what happened. Okay, maybe you will.

John Asked Me To Marry Him! And I said Yes! I would say it again in a heartbeat.

I know we haven't courted for long, but I feel like I've known him for years. And he knows me so well. He makes me laugh and takes me on adventures. He inspires me and helps me and listens to me. He's sweet and funny and handsome and smart. Oh, I don't know if I can describe him accurately! It's nearly impossible to pour everything in my heart onto this paper. Simply put, he's the man of my dreams.

It will be a little while still until we marry, so please don't tell anyone yet. Much longer than the three months since we met. You see, neither of us has yet been baptized into the church, so that adds extra time and preparation. But it doesn't matter. I would gladly wait much longer for him. I know it's not our way to tell, but I thought I would just burst if I didn't share the news with someone.

Magdalena, I don't have the words to describe how wonderful love feels. It's beautiful and amazing and indescribable. I've even been dancing! Not in front of anyone, of course. Oh, I pray you will feel this way someday soon.

I will let you know when our nuptials are to be.

Your friend,

Rosanna

P.S. I'm getting married!!!!!

Chapter Ten

Zach closed his eyes, remembering one of the first conversations he'd had with one of his fellow soldiers.

"Hey, where you from, man?"

Zach looked to his comrade, Jones, who polished his boots. "Kentucky."

"Never been there. What's it like?"

Zachariah pictured his parents' property with all its surrounding trees. "It's beautiful, at least it is where I lived. There are many trees and hills. Everything is green in summer, and in fall you'll see leaves of every color. We get some snow in winter, too, and I really enjoy that. The next farm over is a few miles away, so we're pretty secluded."

"What do you do out there in the sticks, Farm Boy?"

Zachariah chuckled. "Farm Boy, huh? *Jah*, I guess that's pretty accurate. We do have a farm. We grow tobacco and raise horses." He smiled at Jones. "Where are you from?"

He shrugged as though it were of little importance. "California. Hey, you got any family?"

"My folks, two brothers, and two sisters." How he missed them. "You?"

"I have a wife and a little girl. She's two." He pulled out his wallet and showed Zach a photograph. "I can't wait to get back home to them."

"Very nice." He looked forward to the day he'd have a family of his own. He'd hoped that it would be with Rosanna, but he knew that could never happen now.

Jones longingly stared at the photo in his hands before returning it to his wallet. "You know, at first, I didn't really want a kid. But things happen, you know. Selena ended up getting pregnant so we got married. Now, I think those two are the best things that's ever happened to me." Zach noticed a slight misting of his friend's eyes.

Wow, how different their lives had been. It was amazing how each person's story was unique. Yet, here they were working and living side by side as brothers.

"Do you have a picture of your family?"

He shook his head. "No. I came from an Amish community. Photos weren't allowed."

"What? Not allowed? That's crazy, man."

He supposed it did sound pretty strange to an *Englischer* who'd grown up with photographs his whole life. He didn't even attempt to explain.

"Don't you wish you had at least one? That way, you could bring it out and look at their faces once in a while."

Zach shrugged. "I know what they look like."

"Well, to me, having a picture of those I love most makes me remember why I'm here, why I'm fighting." He pointed toward the door behind him with his thumb. "Imagine if those crazies out there tried to take over the world like Hitler or Mussolini, or one of the other psycho nut jobs. That's why we're here, to protect our loved ones from harm."

Zachariah pondered Jones' words. He'd heard a little of Hitler before, but his knowledge of history was dismal. Is that what these soldiers were all here for? To protect their loved ones from harm? How could that be a bad thing?

The story of Jacob Hochstetler and the Indians came to his mind. This man had refused to take up arms against the enemy and it cost him his wife and two of his children. Had he been wrong not to defend his loved ones?

He thought about the story of David and Goliath in the Bible. He couldn't remember God ever condemning David for his actions. On the contrary, He'd called David a man after His own heart. But David had killed the enemy in order to protect his people.

Suddenly, Zach didn't feel so guilty about where he was. Could this be part of God's plan, despite what he'd always been taught?

The intense attack from just days before was still fresh in Zach's mind. His ever-present injury couldn't let him forget it. He did his best to not think about the events that had brought him to this point, nor the grueling days ahead of him.

If he could only get the nightmares to stop. Every time he thought about himself and Jones…he sucked in a breath and quickly wiped away the tears that threatened to brand him as weak. But he hadn't been the only soldier bawling that day. Many in their platoon mourned the life of their comrade and brother.

Tomorrow would be the day they were shipping him out to Germany. He was of no use in his present state. He'd sustained a leg injury that required more medical attention than was available here in Afghanistan.

Zachariah winced as the medic sewed up his wound with temporary sutures. Although the pain paled in comparison to the shrapnel wound being scraped out and closed, just looking at it made him feel queasy. Which made absolutely no sense in Zach's mind. Why was it he could shoot a doe, gut it out, fillet it into pieces, yet when it came to his own flesh and bones, his stomach roiled? Had he gone soft?

"We're going to send you stateside for surgery."

Zach frowned. "Surgery? What do you mean?"

The medic grimaced. "I'm sending you to an orthopedic surgeon. They may have to amputate. We do have good surgeons here in Germany, but I think it would be best if you were closer to home."

"You mean, they're going to cut off part of my leg?" His eyes widened.

Zimmerman touched his shoulder. "Yeah, that's what he means, Farm Boy."

No! I need my leg!

"I'm hoping they won't need to," the medic added.

"But your tibia is pretty much shattered. That's why you've been in so much pain. Don't worry, they can make you a prosthetic leg if need be."

Zach swallowed. "What does that mean?"

"They can design an artificial limb so you can walk normally again. You'll probably need to use crutches for a while, but if you get a prosthesis, you can walk without crutches."

"Can they do something about the pain?"

"I'm going to prescribe some pain meds for you. That should help."

When Zachariah had left the Amish, he never dreamed that he'd return without one of his limbs. What Amish woman would want a husband that couldn't provide for his own? Farm work was by no means easy; it was labor intensive. So how would he be able to operate a farm while in constant pain? He didn't wish to be on pain medication his entire life.

Zachariah stared at the brown bottle in front of him, oblivious to the sights and sounds all around him. What was Rosanna doing right now? Was she busy teaching? Was she correcting her scholars' papers? Was she out with John? How was her folks' house coming along? Did her family still live with his?

"Hey, man, you gonna drink that or just stare at it all night?"

"You can have it." He pushed the beer toward his friend.

"Oh, no. I ordered that for you, buddy. You deserve it."

"Thanks." He shrugged and took a swig. While he'd

never been super fond of drinking, he figured one drink every now and then couldn't hurt. Besides, it helped take his mind off his inner turmoil. The fact that if he returned to the Amish, he'd return home a shunned man. The fact that he'd never have a chance with beautiful Rosanna. The fact that he had to hide his true feelings from his best friend. And the fact that he'd alienated his family and violated his own conscience.

"Another round, please." Sanders called to the waitress and she nodded.

Zach examined his bottle. Was it empty already?

Zach stared at the petite young woman as she set their drinks on the table. She was cute alright, but she didn't come close to Rosanna. He wondered if he'd ever look at another woman without comparing her to Rosanna. Maybe someday he would, but now Rosanna was all he could think about. She filled his dreams at night and distracted him many times throughout the day. He'd hoped that going away would help him to forget about her, but that didn't even seem like a possibility. But he had to, because chances were, she was head-over-heels in love with his best friend by now.

He took the last sip of his beer and realized that, for the first time since the explosion, he had no pain.

"You're going home tomorrow."

Zachariah couldn't believe the officer's words. Home? Already? After three months? He couldn't go home yet. He hadn't been gone long enough.

"Can't I work in the kitchen or sit at a desk or something? I don't want to go home." He never thought he'd hear himself say those words, but his buddies in the military had been like a family to him. They'd become somewhat of a substitute for what he was missing at home. If he left now, he'd have no one.

The officer eyed him with sympathy. "Has the Army taught you nothing? You realize you're arguing with authority, right?"

"No, sir. I'm not arguing, I'm simply putting in a request."

"You're not qualified for either of those positions and besides, they're already filled. What you need to do is thank your lucky stars that you're still alive. Go home and learn to adjust to civilian life. I'll see what I can line up for you as far as a job goes after your surgery and rehabilitation. But it will most likely be months before you've recovered." He sighed. "You've got some tough times ahead of you, but look on the bright side. You still have use of your right leg. That means you can still drive."

Zach grimaced. He'd planned on returning to the Amish once he was done serving his time. Now, he'd be useless on an Amish farm.

"I think I need a drink."

"You deserve one. Just don't overdo it." He handed him his papers. "You are dismissed."

Zachariah tossed and turned all night long with nary a wink. This had to be one of the worst nights of his life. More difficult than the night he'd decided to leave the Amish. How on earth was he going to return home? He'd expected to be gone for at least six months to a year or two. He couldn't face his folks now, especially in his current state. Or anyone, for that matter.

Surely, the Keim family still resided in his home. Or had they been able to move into their own place by now? The Amish did work quickly when it came to important tasks. Either way, there was no way he would go back and face Rosanna—not like this. He had to come up with a plan. He could live on his own, couldn't he? He didn't *have to* return to the Amish. But where would he go?

Chapter Eleven

Rosanna grinned. The day was finally upon them! She helped her family and the Zooks carry their boxed belongings out to the horse-drawn trailer that was awaiting them. They were at last moving out of the Zooks' house and into their own home.

The Keims were all excited about acquiring their own space and getting settled and the Zooks were most likely glad to return to normal life once they departed. Despite the taxing work, smiles abounded as the transition from house to house was made.

She knew her father looked forward to living in a house that belonged to him, while her mother could hardly wait to once again have a kitchen to herself. Margaret, Frances, and Rosanna would return to having their own bedrooms, a pleasant change after the cramped quarters with the Zooks. Much as the families enjoyed one another's company, everyone would be relieved once the move was complete.

After the last of the boxes were deposited inside the

house, Rosanna's father addressed the Zooks. "We cannot thank you enough for your kindness and hospitality these past weeks. It means ever so much to us."

"It was an honor to have you. I praise *Gott* for bringing your family to Kentucky. You have been a great blessing." Abram Zook offered his hand and the two men shook.

They bid the Zooks a goodbye before beginning to unpack—this time for good.

Zach breathed a prayer as his hand poised to knock on the door. Tommy Brooks, one of his fellow soldiers, had been kind enough to suggest a place to stay. It turned out that his folks rented out their garage-turned-studio apartment for a decent price. Since the military still provided income, he had enough to live on.

A woman called through the door. "Who is it?"

"I'm a friend of Brooks. We were in the military together and he told me you rented out your garage."

"Yes, he called and told us you'd be coming." She opened the door wide and smiled. "Any friend of Tommy's is welcome in our home. Come on in and I'll show you the room. How is he doing, by the way?"

"He's doing well."

Her eyes widened when she noticed his crutches. "Your leg! Were you injured?"

"Wounded in battle, ma'am."

"Oh, I'm so sorry." She frowned. "When did you return?"

"Just today, ma'am."

"Oh, where are my manners? I'm Betty, Betty Brooks, Tommy's mom." She offered her hand. "And your name?"

"Uh, Zach. The boys called me Farm Boy." He smiled, remembering when Jones had first given him his nickname.

"Well, it's very good to meet you, Zach. Your mother must be worried sick. Have you contacted her?"

"Uh, no, ma'am."

"You are more than welcome to use our phone."

"My folks don't have a phone. I was Amish before joining the military."

"Oh?"

"Yes, ma'am. And truthfully, my folks probably don't want to see me now." He knew that was only a partial truth. His folks would love to see him, but only under specific circumstances. He'd be expected to return to the Amish and make a kneeling confession—which he was not ready to do at the moment.

"I'm sorry." Her countenance fell. He could tell that she probably had a hundred questions, but to her credit and his relief, she didn't voice any of them. "Well, let me show you to your room now."

She led the way through the house and walked out to a detached garage, which was connected by an outdoor breezeway. "It's not too large, but you have your own bathroom and a kitchenette. I'm sorry we don't have a stove in here, but you can use the hot plate and the toaster oven."

He grimaced. "I've actually never really cooked much, so it will be a learning experience."

"If you'd like, we can include meals for an extra

hundred a month. But it'll only be breakfast and supper—nothing fancy."

"That would be wonderful, ma'am."

"Okay, then. Dinner will be served around six o'clock." She moved to the door. "I'll just leave you to get settled."

"Thank you, ma'am." Just as she was about to close the door, Zach spoke up. "Uh, I hate to ask this, but do you think you can drive me to the hospital next week? I don't have a car and I'm scheduled for surgery."

She eyed him with compassion. "Of course, son. But, are you certain you don't want to contact your family? I know that if Tommy were to be having surgery, I'd want to know."

"*Jah*, I'm sure. See, my folks don't approve of war or of me being a soldier. It's best if they don't know I'm back home for now. I do plan to visit them later."

"Okay, then. If you're sure."

"I am. *Denki.* Uh, thank you."

Zachariah sighed when Betty closed the door, happy to get off his aching leg. The officer was right. It was going to be a tough road.

Rosanna glanced down at her hand in John's and smiled. How blessed she was to have found an honorable man. She'd been counting down the days till their wedding. Lately, though, John had seemed a little melancholy. His usual teasing self was still there, but there had been an underlying despondency that had her concerned about her beau.

"You've been quiet. What's wrong?"

"Just thinking about Zach, is all. I wonder how he's doing."

Rosanna figured that's what it was, but honestly, she didn't have any encouraging words for him.

"I wonder if he's all right. I wonder what kinds of things he's seeing. I miss him."

"He'll be back eventually, right?"

"*Jah.* Our wedding is in a month. I just never thought I'd be getting married without my best friend by my side. I always pictured Zachariah as one of my *new-ehockers*."

"Do you know when he's scheduled to come back?"

"*Nee.* Even so, he wouldn't be allowed to be in our wedding. You know the rules."

"Well, he made the choice to leave and get himself shunned. We all just have to live with it now."

He sighed. "I reckon. He'll probably be under the watchful eye of the leaders for months after he returns. Who knows how long it would be before they lift the *Bann*."

Chapter Twelve

John picked up the can of spray paint he'd been eyeing, then glanced to the next aisle. The guy reminded him a lot of Zach, but he wore a baseball cap and had short hair. His jeans and black t-shirt bearing an eagle with an American flag told John he was clearly an *Englischer*. How he missed his good friend. He couldn't help but wish he was here.

He glanced at the guy again and did a double take. *No way!*

"Zach? Zachariah Zook, is that you?" He rushed over to his friend and engulfed him in a bear hug. "I almost didn't recognize you with the short hair and *Englisch* clothes."

"Yep, it's me."

"You look so…so *Englisch*." He laughed and clasped Zach's shoulder. "How are you, my good friend?"

"I'm still alive."

"What happened? Why are you here?"

He pointed to a pair of crutches in the shopping cart. "Bum leg. They sent me back early."

"Oh, no. You were injured?" John ran a hand through his hair. "Why haven't you come home? Why didn't you get a hold of me?"

"I don't want to ruin your life."

"*Ruin* my life? Are you kidding?" He looked at Zach's cart again. *Beer?* "Hey, what's that all about? You here shopping with someone else?"

"Nope. It's all mine." He grimaced.

"Two cases?"

"Aren't I lucky?"

"Zach, you're drinking now?"

"Looks like it. Wanna join me?"

"Uh, no. Rosie, would—"

"Ah, the illustrious Rosanna Keim."

Illustrious? "Soon to be Christner. We're getting married this month."

"Already, huh?" Zach's eyes widened. "Congratulations, man. So you got her to say yes?"

"Yeah, I had to twist her arm a bit but she eventually agreed."

Zach's brow shot up.

"Joke." John grinned.

"Yeah."

Why was this conversation so awkward? Zach seemed so different. What had happened to the Zachariah he knew? "Hey, why don't you come over for supper one of these nights?"

"With your folks?"

"Sure."

He shook his head. "No. I'm not going back."

"What do you mean?"

"What's there for me, John? Ridicule? Condemnation? In case you haven't noticed, I have enough to deal with right now."

"You know your folks love you."

"My folks have to do what they have to do, love or no. You know I won't be welcomed."

He put a hand on Zach's arm. "I'm sorry, for everything."

"What are friends for?" He glanced back at his cart. "Hey, you got any plans? Want to come hang out?"

John wasn't about to miss an opportunity to spend time with Zach. "Sure. Where?"

"My place. Well, not *my* place exactly. I'm renting a studio apartment."

"Great."

Zach's face lit up for the first time. "You'll have to leave your buggy here and ride with me. It's a little ways."

"I came with a driver. Old Ernie. I'll just let him know I already have a ride home."

"Okay."

Rosanna watched the clock on the wall. *Where could he be?* John said he'd be there to pick her up from school today. Perhaps he'd forgotten. Not a problem, she could walk home if she had to. Unfortunately, the walk home was longer now than when her family resided with the Zooks.

She sighed in disappointment. John had never broken his word.

Hopefully, nothing was wrong. She sent up a silent prayer on his behalf.

* * *

"You said you needed to be home at what time?"

John didn't miss the slur in Zach's words as he spoke. He'd tried to get Zach to stop at two beers, to no avail. He wondered just how many his friend drank on a normal basis.

He looked up at the clock and grimaced. "Two hours ago."

Zach set his bottle down on the table beside him, stood up and jingled his keys. "Let's go."

"No. You're not going anywhere tonight, buddy."

"Ah." He swatted the air in front of him. "I can drive."

"Yep. Right into a tree. Then where would we be?"

"You *chust* gonna crash here then?"

"Looks like it. It's preferable to a telephone pole." He looked around. There wasn't much room in the tiny apartment but it was plenty sufficient for one occupant. "I'll sleep on your chair. Got an extra blanket?"

"On the couch."

"Thanks, friend." He took the blanket and made himself as comfortable as possible as he reclined on the chair. He turned out the lamp on the table next to him. "Hey, Zach. Do me a favor and don't drink any alcohol tomorrow morning. I need to get home."

His friend put his hand to his brow and offered a halfhearted salute. "Yes, sir."

John sighed as he thought about the state of his best friend. He was glad they'd had an opportunity to talk before Zach became intoxicated. The war had been tough, although John knew there was much more to it than what Zach had shared with him. He couldn't believe his friend had nearly lost his leg in battle. The more he thought about it, the more his heart ached for him. Zach needed help and support, and he was determined to give it to him.

The Brookses had, no doubt, been a Godsend to Zach. The way Zach talked about them sounded as if they were his folks. They'd visited him in the hospital, helped him to purchase a car, assisted him with his physical therapy, provided meals, and the list went on.

John bowed his head in silent prayer and thanked God for keeping his best friend alive and sending people to help him along the way. He prayed that God would show him how he could best help his friend in the days, weeks, and months ahead. And he asked God to let Zach find peace.

Rosanna glanced out the schoolhouse window. Had she heard the rumble of a vehicle outside?

She bent down and whispered into her most responsible student's ear. "I'll be right back, Fannie. Keep an eye on everyone. Make sure nobody gets up from their desk." Fortunately, they were all busy with a reading assignment.

At the girl's nod, Rosanna headed outside.

She took a step toward the vehicle as John stepped out of the passenger's side door. It sure was good to see him.

She smiled, finally able to dismiss her fears from earlier. "John? Where have you been?"

The driver's door opened, drawing her attention, and a young *Englisch* man stepped out.

John smiled at Rosanna and took her hand. "Surprise!" He looked to the driver.

She stared at the driver a little closer. Did she know him? It wasn't until he removed his baseball cap and moved his sunglasses to his head that she realized who it was.

"Zachariah Zook?" Her jaw dropped.

"I found him in town yesterday. Can you believe it?"

"Hey, Rosanna." Zach nodded.

Rosanna swallowed the bile that threatened to rise in her throat. How could John just show up out of the blue with Zachariah of all people? Didn't he realize Zach's sisters were inside the schoolhouse? The same sisters who'd taken abuse from the other scholars because of their older brother's foolish choices?

"I—I have to go back inside."

John frowned and lightly grasped her wrist. "Rosie? Aren't you happy to see Zach?"

"*Jah.* Just thrilled." She turned and marched back to the schoolhouse. At the steps, she turned to face them again, pinning John with a look that could cause a sinkhole in the ground. "It would probably be best if the two of you left now."

Ouch. John grimaced.

"*That's* the reaction I expected." Zachariah slipped back into his car with as much finesse one could have with an injured leg.

John frowned as he sat back into the passenger's seat. *How could Rosanna be so rude to Zach?* "Not exactly the warm welcome you hoped for, huh?" He attempted to make light of the situation.

"Who can blame her?" He turned the engine over and they headed in the direction of John's house.

"She's never acted that way before. I guess you really bring out the best in people." He hoped that a joke would lighten the mood a little.

"Okay." Zach threw his hands up in surrender. "I have a confession to make. There's another reason she doesn't like me."

John's brow lifted. "What? Did you run her cat over with your buggy?"

Zach chuckled. "Close."

"Um…let's see. You threw her prayer *kapp* out in the rain and ruined it?"

Zach shook his head. "Worse. Maybe I should have you agree to not clobbering me before I tell you this."

"Too late. Speak."

"I kissed her."

John's gaze turned serious.

He held up a hand. "Let me reword that. I attempted to kiss her."

"I think I *should* clobber you."

"Let me explain a little better. *Before* she met you and the Keims were living at our, or I should say, my folks' place, I sort of made a pass at her."

"Oh. It was before?" He shrugged. "Well, I guess I can't say that I blame you. She *is* beautiful." He tossed a look of warning. "And she *is* mine now."

"I totally get it. That was one of the reasons I readily joined the military. I didn't want to get in the way."

John felt his brow sprout up. "So, she *didn't* kiss you back?"

Zach laughed. It was good to see him more like his old self. "Are you kidding me? I think she wanted to knock the daylights out of me."

"Really?"

"Yeah. Her father did too."

"So you just gave up?"

"Truthfully, when you came along and showed an interest in her, I kinda let you have her—not that it was *all* my choice. But I did stop pursuing her."

"Why would you do that?"

"Well, remember how you always talked about leaving the Amish?"

He nodded.

"I thought Rosanna would be a good reason for you to stay. I didn't want to lose my best friend to the world." He chuckled. "It's ironic, isn't it? *I'm* the one who's *Englisch* now."

"You don't have to be, you know?"

He shook his head. "I don't know if I'll make a good Amish man now. I can't farm with this leg. What would I do?"

John shrugged. "I'm sure there's probably something you can do." He thought for a moment, but his mind came up blank. Zach was right. What could an Amish man with an injured leg do? It's not like he could just secure an office job and utilize a computer all day.

John squeezed his friend's shoulder. "You know, you really are the best friend a guy could ever buy...er, uh, have." He chuckled at his joke.

Zach laughed out loud.

"But, seriously, Zach. I mean it."

Zach's brow arched. "Really?"

"Well, yeah. I wouldn't have said it otherwise."

Zachariah put his hand on John's shoulder. "Thanks, man, it means a lot."

Chapter Thirteen

"John?"

John turned at his father's voice. "*Jah, Dat?*"

"Where have you been?"

"Just spent the night with a friend in town, is all."

His father's brow rose. "Not with Rosanna Keim, I hope."

Heat shot up John's neck at his father's insinuation. "*Nee.* We are not married yet."

His father blew out a relieved breath and pointed down the road where Zach's car had been a few moments ago. "An *Englischer?*"

"*Jah.*"

His father's intense gaze bore down on him. "Was it Zachariah Zook?"

John frowned. Zach hadn't wanted anyone to know he was back in town, but how could he possibly dodge his father's direct question? He swallowed. "*Jah.*"

"He is in the *Bann*. It is not wise to spend time with him." His father stroked his beard. "You do not want to add any problems that will prevent your wedding to Rosanna Keim."

"I know."

"Will he make a kneeling confession?"

"I don't know, *Dat*." John finally blew out the breath that threatened to burst his lungs.

"Best you stay away from that Zook boy."

John nodded and paused to see if his father had anything else to say. When he remained silent, John continued to his bedroom. It appeared Zach's return wasn't going to be easy on anybody.

A pothole in the road startled John out of his musings. He shook his head and refocused on the path ahead of him—the road that led to the one-room schoolhouse he'd grown up in.

What would Rosie say when he picked her up today? If her earlier tone was any indication, he was in for a tongue lashing. He hoped it wouldn't be so, but at the same time he was excited to talk to Rosie about Zach. His friend had returned!

He slowly pulled up to the schoolhouse. Like other days, he would wait until Rosie came out to meet him. Hopefully, she wouldn't be too long today. He'd only been gone a day, but it seemed much longer. Why was it that when you were away from the one you loved, the days seemed to go on forever? And then, by contrast, the time you had with them never lasted long enough.

His countenance brightened when she emerged at the top of the steps.

She silently walked to his buggy and sat in the passenger's seat. She kept her gaze on the driving mare. Would she say nothing the entire ride home?

He'd have to start the conversation today. The tension in the air made him uneasy and he guessed the same was true with Rosie, so he'd do his best to minimize it. "How was school?"

"Fine."

"Have I ever told you that you look cute when you're upset?"

"If you're attempting to get me to laugh, it's not working. No one looks *gut* when they're mad."

"Not laugh. I just want you to open up to me." He lightly touched her hand. "I'm guessing you're upset about Zach's return?"

"Return? So he's back for *gut*?"

John frowned. "Not exactly."

"He's staying *Englisch* then?"

"I think he's still in the military. He's just not on active duty. He was injured over in Afghanistan. You probably didn't notice, but his leg is messed up pretty bad. The doctors attempted to fix it with surgery, but there was too much damage. They said he was lucky to still have it. He will most likely never be able to walk like he used to and will probably endure back problems as a result."

Rosanna nodded. "If he's not coming back, why did you bring him here?"

"He gave me a ride." He shook his head. "Look, Rosie, Zachariah Zook is my best friend. I want to do what I can to help him."

"Help him?"

John sighed. Was it really a good idea to tell Rosie about Zach's drinking? *No, that can wait for another time.* "I want to be his friend."

"You know we are not to have fellowship with fence jumpers." She frowned. "Is that why you didn't pick me up last night?"

He rubbed the back of his neck. "Uh…*jah*. We hung out at his place." Hopefully, she wouldn't ask any more questions. He wouldn't tell her why he couldn't come home the prior evening. They'd jump over one bale of hay at a time.

"And you returned this morning?"

"If Zach is ever going to return home for *gut*, I think he needs contact with our people." He locked eyes with her. He might as well confess. "I invited him to our wedding."

Her gaze widened and she looked away. "Why?"

John noticed her eyes misting and he knew he had to tread lightly here. "*Schatzi*, please try to understand. Zach is the closest friend I've had since my first day of school. We've done practically everything together. I love him just as much as I would a brother, maybe more. I won't turn my back on him. How could I not invite him to one of the most important events in my life? Even if he can't be my *newehocker*, I still want him to share the day with us."

"You know a soldier won't be welcomed among our people. And what about his folks? Will he contact them before the wedding?"

"I don't know, but I can understand your concern. I'll suggest that to Zach."

"My *vatter* won't like it that you're spending time with Zachariah Zook."

"Then don't tell him."

"Word will get around, you know it always does."

"If it does, I'll talk to him. Don't worry, Rosie. Everything's gonna turn out just fine, okay? Trust me?"

"I guess I have to."

"*Gut*." He reached over and took her hand. "Let's talk about something else."

A timid knock sounded from outside Zach's door on Sunday morning.

He made his way to the entrance and opened it to see Betty Brooks, his landlady.

She smiled. "Good morning, Zach. Frank and I were wondering if you would like to attend church with us this morning. You are more than welcome to join us."

Church? He'd never attended an *Englisch* worship service. "Well… No, thank you, ma'am. I…don't think I'm ready for church yet."

"Oh." Her countenance dimmed a bit. "Well, if you change your mind, it's just down the road a few miles, on the left. Crossroads Baptist Church. You can't miss it.

"And the offer stands for any Sunday, as well. Just let us know if you'd like to join us. We have a wonderful pastor, lots of young people around your age, and…" she hesitated, "they offer a Reformers Unanimous program too. It's for people with addictions."

Zach understood the woman's reservations. Though she hadn't said a thing, he knew she disapproved of his drinking habit. He suspected he'd have been asked to leave for that reason, were he not Tommy's friend.

"Thank you for the offer, Mrs. Brooks. Perhaps I will come someday."

Now that he thought of it, hadn't John mentioned trying to find a good *Englisch* church? Maybe he should go once or twice to appease his best friend. He'd think about it.

Chapter Fourteen

A smile played on Rosanna's lips as she sprayed the dress sleeve then ran the hot iron over it. Tomorrow was the day! A day she'd looked forward to since childhood. She hadn't known then that she'd be getting married at age eighteen, but here she was. She'd always pictured herself older.

She thought of her teaching position and the impact her leaving would have on the children. She'd miss them for sure and for certain. The leaders had said she could keep the job for as long as she wanted, with her husband's permission and provided she wasn't in the family way.

Rosanna picked up her wedding dress and eyed it with satisfaction. This was the first dress she'd had in this particular color, a deep turquoise. It wouldn't have been allowed in the Miller Amish. She loved the new-found freedom Honey Ridge afforded, but somehow she felt certain things were wrong. How did it make sense that things that were *verboten* in her former church were suddenly okay now that they were in Honey Ridge? It was as though the leaders had more say than God did. Or had the leaders from her other district not been listening to God? Either way, it seemed like everything was subject to the leaders' opinions. After all, had God said in the Bible somewhere that certain colors of dress were not acceptable? She'd never seen a reference to it. She knew she shouldn't be thinking this way, questioning the leaders, but sometimes she couldn't quiet these protests in her head.

She'd done a *gut* job making her wedding dress. It was no doubt her best yet, not that she would admit it to anyone. *Nee*, that would be *hochmut*. But her sewing skills had definitely improved. *Mamm* had been reviewing pants-making with her as of late. Since *Dat* was the only male in the family, she hadn't had much experience making broadfall trousers. It would be a necessary skill as a wife.

Her mind travelled to John and the past year of her life. What an adventure it had been, moving to a new place, finding a new love, and moving into a new home. Everything seemed to happen in a whirlwind and here she was facing her wedding day.

What a blessed woman she was to be marrying a man like John. Handsome, hardworking, kind, and funny... what else could she ask for? There was no doubt in her mind that he would treat her right. And she knew that *Der Herr* had orchestrated their first encounter. Why else would they have moved in with the Zooks? *Jah*, it was God's will for sure and certain.

Magdalena would be arriving tonight with a group

of other folks from her former district and she couldn't wait. It would be so *gut* to see her best friend again. She couldn't help but hope that Magdalena would move down to Kentucky too someday.

She and John had already been talking about match-making Magdalena with one of their friends or brothers. John had mentioned Zach, which was absolutely out of the question as far as Rosanna was concerned. The last thing she wanted was her best friend with Zachariah Zook. What a miserable cursed life she'd have. Even if Zach returned, there was no way she'd suggest they get together.

Why did Zach have to leave and ruin everything? It seemed that John couldn't take his mind off his way-ward friend. She regretted the fact that John couldn't have his best friend participate in his wedding, but there was no way around it. In fact, the leaders would most likely look down on Zachariah's attendance. At the very least, he'd have to sit at a table separate from the other Amish folks. Was it possible that Zachariah could actu-ally acclimate to the Amish culture after he'd been out in the world? Rosanna didn't think so. If she were hon-est with herself, she'd probably have a pretty difficult time going back to her former district and their strin-gent ways—and she was still Amish. No, the chances of Zach's return were slim to none and slim just left town, as John would say.

John carried the folding bench to the Keims' liv-ing room and pulled the stabilizing legs down on each side. He eyed the other men bringing in the benches, his brothers and Zach's, and his heart couldn't help but ache for his best friend. Planning for a wedding in his absence seemed less fulfilling somehow. When you'd always pictured things a certain way, and then they ended up being different, disappointment invariably set in.

He'd called Zach from the phone shanty yesterday and his friend promised he'd be at the wedding. That was the most he could hope for in their current situation, which was entirely his own fault. Well, not *entirely*, but it sure felt that way. He'd hoped that reconnecting with Zach would encourage him to stop drinking, but there had been no change as of yet. Every time he visited his friend, the fridge never lacked a decent supply of alcohol.

A commotion drew his attention outside. He heard Rosanna's voice and peeked out the window. Just as he surmised, the folks from Indiana had arrived. Truth be known, he'd been nervous all day about meeting them. These were people Rosie had grown up with. Would they approve of her choice of a husband? Would he be good enough to meet their expectations?

"John, come." He heard Rosie beckon from the backyard.

He hastily tossed the rag that he'd been using to dust the bench onto the floor, and wiped his sweaty hands on his pants. He moved outside as quickly as possible. Since Rosie had said the district she was from was small, he'd expected a few people, but not four passenger vans full. Apparently, Rosie had a lot of family or their family had a plethora of friends.

Rosie introduced John to Magdalena and a few of her cousins.

John nodded and shook their hands. "I see the Miller District has its share of pretty *maed*."

Rosanna nudged him and smiled at her friends. "See, I told you he was a charmer."

"I just call it like it is." He winked at Rosanna.

Rosanna and Magdalena shared a smile, which John guessed was Magdalena's approval of Rosanna's choice in a mate. He currently wondered just how much Rosie's friend already knew about him.

"Well, if y'all don't mind, I better get back inside. There's a lot to do if we want to be ready by tomorrow." He eyed his bride-to-be. "And you, sweet Rosie, will need to turn in at a decent hour if we're to be prepared for all the festivities tomorrow."

A splash of color painted her cheeks. "Don't you worry. I'll have plenty of energy tomorrow, even if the girls and I stay up talking all night."

He looked longingly into her eyes before disappearing into the house. Tomorrow!

"Oh, my. I think we're almost done. And it's a good thing because I think I'm nearing a collapse from exhaustion." Rosanna walked into the main room of the house.

"We can't have that, can we?" John's gaze met his future wife's.

She smiled. "It's tomorrow. Can you believe it?"

"Oh yeah, I can believe it. It will be the best day of my life for sure and certain." He moved closer and motioned her near. He eyed her lips and raised his brow.

"What?" She grinned and gently bit down on her bottom lip. How he enjoyed the longing look in her eye.

"Oh, you know exactly what," he whispered in her ear, and then nuzzled just below it. His lips softly caressed her neck and a slight gasp escaped her lips. He met her mouth with such intensity, he briefly worried he might have brushed her chin with his stubble and left a burn. When Rosie's fingers wove through the hair at the nape of his neck, his hesitation fled away. Her feminine form pressed against him and left him longing with a desire that would soon be fulfilled. Very soon.

"Hey, where did you—" Magdalena stopped dead in her tracks.

John and Rosanna sprang apart as quickly as possible, both desperately attempting to reclaim their breath and steady their hearts. He really should have been more aware of potential interruptions, but the temptation of kissing his beloved had been too great. At least it was just Rosie's friend and not one of the leaders or their folks.

Her friend must've turned five shades of pink. "Oh, I—I'm sorry, I'll just come back later." Magdalena disappeared from the room in short order.

John laughed and intertwined his fingers with Rosanna's. He pulled her close and gazed longingly into the depths of her eyes. "Perhaps we should continue this conversation at a later date?"

"Perhaps." Color blossomed on Rosie's cheeks. He couldn't wait to see more of that look in the near future. He hadn't felt that much passion from Rosanna since she'd attacked him on the side of the road. Granted, it was a most welcomed attack that he'd secretly wished she'd execute again. But, he'd determined to move at the pace she preferred. They'd be married tomorrow, and that meant it would be just a few more days when they could fully consummate their love. This kiss was just a teaser, but also a promise of amazing things to come. Meeting Rosanna Keim had no doubt been the best fortune he'd ever stumbled upon. What a blessed man he was to have a woman like her.

Rosanna was just about to prepare for bed when a familiar knock came from her door. "Come in," she said quietly, plopping down cross-legged onto her bed.

Magdalena entered her bedroom and closed the door. "What was all that I saw? You never told me about any of that," she teased.

Heat cradled her cheeks. "You can't really write about things of that nature in a letter."

Magdalena's gaze turned serious. "But, you and John haven't…done anything that needs to be repented of, have you?"

She blushed again. "No, of course not. What you saw today was actually the farthest it's ever gone," she admitted.

"Good." Mischief lit her best friend's eyes. "So does he taste as sweet as he looks?"

Rosanna gasped in shock. "Magdalena! Shh…he's just in the other room. What if he heard you?"

"What? It's a simple question." Despite her words, her cheeks darkened a bit, as though surprised by her own audacity. "Perhaps he has a good-looking brother looking for an *aldi*?" She flicked an imaginary piece of lint off her dress. "I wouldn't mind moving down here and living close to my best friend."

"*Ach*, Magdalena, I would love that!" Rosanna squeezed her friend's hands. "You would love Kentucky. It's so beautiful here."

"You still haven't answered my question."

"Which one?"

"Does he taste as good as he looks?"

"*Ach*!" She tossed a pillow at her friend. "I'll never tell!"

They both giggled and Rosanna realized how much she'd missed her best friend, and how happy she was that Magdalena was here now. Tomorrow would be a day that would change both of their lives forever. Rosanna wished that they could remain best friends, no matter what the future held for them.

Chapter Fifteen

The ticking of the clock seemed to grow louder and louder in John's ears. Bishop Hershberger continued his traditional wedding message citing Biblical examples of marriages throughout history. He did his utmost to listen to the Bishop's words, but worrisome thoughts clouded his mind. *Where is Zach?* If his friend didn't arrive soon, he'd miss their taking of vows. *He promised he'd be here.*

Rosanna's eyes met his and he knew she read the concern in them. It wasn't fair to Rosie that her husband-to-be not be fully present in all his faculties. He couldn't help it though. He needed his best friend here to witness his vows. He released an inward sigh and refocused his attention on Rosanna. This *would* be a *wunderbaar* day whether Zachariah was here or not. Nevertheless, he yearned for the former.

John turned at what he was certain to be the creak of a door opening. It had to be Zach. Commotion rose in the congregation and John heard whispers as his friend entered the room and moved toward the front. The bishop frowned at the disruption and quieted for a moment. John offered his bride a reassuring smile.

Zachariah stopped mid-aisle and dropped to his knees.

John frowned. *What on earth is he doing?*

"I'm here to make my kneeling confession, Bishop Hershberger," Zach hollered in his drunken state.

John looked at his best friend in dismay. "Now's not the time, Zach."

"Rosanna! I'm sorry for kissing you the first day you came to Honey Ridge," he slurred.

John glanced at Rosie and he was sure her cheeks nearly turned red as the bulbs on the Christmas tree he'd seen down at the hardware store. He wasn't sure if it was from embarrassment or anger. "*Nee*, Zach!"

"I know I must've killed at least five people in Afghanistan—"

"That's enough! Leave at once, Zachariah," the bishop commanded.

Abram Zook and Zach's younger brother approached Zach and grasped his arms. They began escorting Zach out of the service and John could hear some of their conversation in *Deitsch*.

"Will you shame your family and your best friend at his wedding?" Abram's subdued voice carried over the people.

John looked to Rosanna, who now had tears in her eyes. "I'm sorry," he mouthed.

She nodded and he gently squeezed her hands.

The ceremony continued, but John knew neither one

of them experienced the full joy their wedding should have afforded. While he'd usually be ecstatic about the festivities ahead, a deep sorrow settled in his heart. He knew Zach's leaving had been his own fault. *He* was the reason Zach was in his current state.

After the main ceremony finished, Abram approached him and Rosanna at the *Eck* and apologized for his son's behavior. He informed John that he'd hired a driver to take Zachariah back to his house.

"Thank you, Abram. I feel better now knowing Zach is safe." John nodded.

"You are a *gut* friend to him, John."

"And I will continue to be," he assured.

Was there a look of admiration in Abram's eyes? Perhaps it was appreciation.

He turned to Rosanna as Abram walked away. Rosanna frowned.

"You look sad, *schatzi*. Is everything okay?" He brought her hand to his lips and kissed it. "I *am* sorry about Zach."

"Me too." Her eyes locked with his and he caught her concern. "But I worry about *you*."

"You don't need to."

"What if Zachariah leads you astray? What if…?" Her voice trailed off, but John knew what she was thinking.

"I promise you that will not happen. Rosanna Christner, you are stuck with me the rest of our days whether you like it or not," he teased, wagging his finger at her.

Rosanna fought to keep herself from laughing.

"Now, there's the girl I married." He leaned over and

kissed her cheek. "Let's talk about more pleasant conversation now, shall we?"

Rosie nodded with a smile.

Although he'd meant the words, he couldn't help but
worry about what Zach was doing right now. For Rosie's
sake, he'd keep his anxious thoughts to himself. This
day had already undergone its share of reparation; he
would add no more sadness.

They continued to greet their guests as they came
to their table one by one to offer their congratulations.
For the most part, the guests seemed to act like nothing
had happened as far as Zachariah's unwelcomed out-
burst was concerned. For this, John was thankful but he
was also saddened. How would Zach ever get the help
he needed if those who knew him best and loved him
most pretended like he didn't exist?

John stormed into Zachariah's apartment and
marched straight to the refrigerator. He ignored Zach
sitting on the couch with a beer in his hand.

"Hey, man. What are you doing?"

He pulled a case of beer from the bottom shelf and
set it on the counter next to the sink. "Something I
should have done the first time I came over." He opened
one of the bottles.

"Sure, you can have one." Zach shrugged.

John continued opening bottles and then began
dumping them down the drain.

"Hey, what are you doing?" Zach leaped off the
couch and charged toward him.

"I told you."

"No! Don't dump my beer. I paid a lot of money for that." He grasped John's arm.

John took another bottle with his free hand and began dumping it out. "This garbage is ruining your life."

"No." Zach grabbed the bottle from his hand and John turned at the stench of alcohol on his breath. He looked over to the side table near the couch where his friend had been sitting and counted four empty bottles.

John's eyes bored into Zach's. "Let me do this, Zach."

"I need it," he cried in desperation.

"No, you don't need it. What you need is your family. Come back to our people, Zach."

"You know I can't."

"Do you consider me a friend?"

"You know I do." He released his grasp.

"Then, why in the world did you show up to my wedding drunk?"

Zach scratched his head. "Drunk?"

"You don't even remember?" John shook his head. "Well, let me refresh your memory. You walked into the Keims' house during the ceremony and began confessing every wrong thing you've ever done in your life, including kissing my wife! Does that sound familiar?" He wondered if Zach was even sober enough to grasp the meaning of his words.

"I just had a few beers." Obviously he was not.

He'd have to have a heart to heart chat with his friend when he was sober. It would do no good now. "No more. Go sit back down."

"But that's my beer."

He took several bottles at once and emptied them

into the sink. "No, this is the devil's beer and it's going back to Hell where it came from!"

"Stop it!" Zach lunged at John, pushing him into the side of the fridge. His back arched with pain.

"I'm not going to fight you, if that's what you're trying to start. But I'm also not going to sit back and let you ruin your life." He seized the bottle in his friend's hand and threw it into the sink. He didn't care about the broken glass; that could be cleaned up later.

"My life is already ruined."

"No, it's not. You have your whole life ahead of you, Zach. You can meet a nice girl, get married and settle down. You can still have a great life."

"It's too late."

"No, it's not."

Zach pointed to the empty beer bottles. "You know I'm going to buy more."

John crossed his arms over his chest. "No, you are not."

"You can't stop me."

"Try me," he challenged. "I'll tie you up if I have to."

John watched as Zach defiantly marched past him and out the door. He smirked as his friend attempted to get into his car.

Zach came back into the house. "Forgot my keys." He walked over to the table where he usually kept his wallet and keys and frowned at the empty space. "What's going on, man?"

"You're not going anywhere."

"Who are you, Bishop Hershberger?"

"I'm your friend. Quite possibly the only one you have right now."

"What? So you're just going to sit here and baby-sit me?"

"Looks like it."

"Why?"

"Because I love you and I care about you. Why else would I leave my wife all alone the day after I married her?"

"Rosanna. She's a perty girl, John."

"I know. She's my wife."

Zach looked at him as though a new revelation struck him. "Your wife?"

John sighed. "Yes, Zach. Rosie is my wife now."

"Aw, man. When was the wedding? Why didn't you invite me?"

"I did." He frowned. Although frustrated, John was glad Zach was slowly beginning to sober up. "We'll talk about it later, okay? I'll tell you all about it after you've had a good night's sleep."

"But it's morning," he protested.

"Look outside, buddy."

Zach limped to the window and moved the curtain. "It's dark out there."

"Yep. Bedtime." John pointed to Zach's bed and his friend reluctantly did as told.

John stared at the ceiling for the next two hours before drifting off to sleep. He listened to Zach's snore while his thoughts bounced back and forth between his new wife and his best friend. If he could just get Zach sober and talk him into rejoining the church, it would be just like old times. Zach could find a nice Amish girl to marry, they could build a house on the property next to the acreage he'd purchased for his and Rosie's house, and they could raise their children side-by-side. Who knows, maybe their children would someday end up getting hitched.

Jah, that is a good goal. John smiled as he envisioned their future lives, full of hope and promise.

John grinned as Zach hobbled into the small breakfast nook. He'd managed to find a couple slices of bread and few eggs in Zach's near empty fridge.

"Smells…interesting." Zach checked the fridge then closed it again. Had he been looking for beer?

"You know, you should really be using your crutches."

Zach nodded halfheartedly. "Probably, but I'm trying to learn to walk with just my prosthesis."

John had watched him attach his prosthetic leg earlier and wondered if he would have been the one with a missing limb, had he gone to war.

"Aw, man. My foot itches!"

John shrugged. "So scratch it."

"Not *that* foot, the one that's missing."

John's brow shot up. "What? You mean, your *missing* foot itches?"

Zach chuckled. "Yep. And sometimes my shin hurts like crazy. Phantom pain. Pretty weird, huh?"

"Strange." John moved the plate in front of Zach. "Eat up. We're leaving soon."

"Leaving?"

"I'm taking you home with me," John insisted. "I had one of the *Englisch* drivers bring your car and drop it off. His wife picked him up."

Zach nodded slowly as though not fully comprehending the situation.

"You left it at the Keims' when you came to our wedding. An *Englischer* brought you home."

"How did it go?"

"What? The wedding?" John handed his friend a glass of juice. He grimaced. "It was a disaster, but I managed to salvage as much of it as I could."

His brow shot up. "Disaster?"

"You showed up drunk." His eyes narrowed.

"Oh, no." Zach slapped his forehead with his palm.

"Oh, yes. Zach, it has to stop. You're going to end up ruining your life."

"My life's fine."

"No, it's not. When you show up to your best friend's wedding drunk and humiliate your family, I assure you, your life is *not* fine." He stared at his friend. "I mean it, Zach. This isn't a game."

"I'm sorry."

"Then prove it by getting sober. Don't buy any more alcohol."

He shrugged. "Okay."

"Do you mean it?"

"Yes."

John smiled. This was better news than anything he could have hoped for.

Chapter Sixteen

Rosanna frowned when she looked out the window and saw both John and Zachariah heading toward the house. She'd been looking forward to John's return all morning, but she hadn't expected Zach at his side. She just finished putting the last clean breakfast dish away when the two of them walked through the door.

"Rosie?"

How she loved hearing her name on her husband's lips.

"I'm back, *schatzi*," John called from the door.

"In the kitchen."

He walked through the back mudroom and into the kitchen of her parents' home. The moment he saw her, his grin widened along with his steps toward her. John approached and in one quick moment whisked her into his arms and offered the kiss she'd been dreaming about since he'd left yesterday. Before they got carried away, a throat being cleared reminded them they weren't alone.

John reluctantly broke away. "Oh yeah. Rosie, look what the cat dragged in."

Her gaze momentarily flitted toward Zachariah and she nodded briefly.

Zach stepped forward. "I'd like to apologize for my behavior at the wedding."

Rosanna looked at John, who signaled she should acknowledge his apology. "Okay."

"Okay?" Zach brow shot up. "What exactly does that mean?"

John put his arm around her. "I think that means she forgives you, but she's still a little upset about it." He looked to her. "Am I right?"

She nodded.

"I guess I'll have to take whatever I can get." Zach frowned.

"Rosie, do you think your folks will mind if Zach stays the night?"

Rosanna bit her tongue. How could he even ask such a question? Tonight was supposed to be *their* night. Not theirs *and* Zach's. She'd been craving time with John and wanted him all to herself. She was tired of sharing her husband. It seemed in the time they were married, he'd spent just as much time with Zachariah as he had with her. It just didn't seem fair. He was supposed to be home with her. They were supposed to be building a life together. First, Zachariah wanted to ruin their wedding. Now, he wanted to steal their precious time together?

Rosanna quickly turned back to the sink so the two men wouldn't see the tears gathering in her eyes. She did her best to swallow them back before speaking. She measured her words. "You may ask my father."

"We'll do that." John kissed her head lightly, then disappeared with his best friend at his side.

Rosanna sucked in a deep breath and whispered a desperate plea for help, but what she really felt like doing was screaming.

Concern had been mounting since the moment John returned home with Zach. Something wasn't right with Rosie and he was determined to find out what it was. The last thing he wanted was an argument. This had only been their third day of marriage. He'd stayed long enough to help with all the cleanup from their wedding but missed their second day altogether, because of his time helping Zach sober up.

Now that they were alone in Rosie's folks' *dawdi haus,* they'd be able to spend some time together. His wife had already gone to bed, and he guessed it was because she was upset with him. He quickly undressed and slid into bed next to her.

"Rosie?" his voice was gentle. "Wanna talk?"

His wife shrugged but didn't turn to him.

Yep, she's mad. "What can I do to make things right?" He stroked her soft hair, which evidently had just been shampooed by the subtle sweet fragrance.

Rosanna shrugged.

"Turn to me, please," he requested.

She did as bidden.

He felt the warm moisture on her face. "You're crying, *lieb*? Why?" What on earth had he done to make his bride cry? He needed to come up with something quickly. "I'm not that ugly, am I?"

Her shoulders shook and he knew he'd struck a chord. "You're not supposed to try to make me laugh when I'm crying. It's just not right."

"But I don't want you to cry. I hate seeing you cry."

"Why is Zachariah here?"

"I don't want him staying alone at his apartment. He'll just go buy more beer."

"Are you planning on having him move in with us?"

"No. Of course, not. It's just temporary. If he dries out and sees that he doesn't need the alcohol, I'm hoping he'll stop drinking."

"How long is he staying?"

"I don't know. A few days, maybe. I'm hoping he'll go back home to his folks' place."

"We're supposed to leave tomorrow, remember?"

He smacked his forehead with his palm. "Ah, man. I forgot all about that. Can it wait a few days?"

"We have people expecting us, John." He heard the exasperation in her voice and he knew she was on the verge of crying again. "Do you not want to go?"

"*Nee, lieb.* Of course, I want to go. It's just…" He thought about it for a moment. "I'll talk to Abram Zook tomorrow and see if Zach can stay with them. If he agrees, you and I can go. If not, we'll have to postpone it a few more days. Is that okay with you?"

"I guess it has to be, *jah*?"

"I just want to help Zach. I want to see him living his life like he should. If it were me, wouldn't *you* do the same?"

"*Jah.*"

"Maybe Zach's cousin Elam will help him out. He

still lives with his folks, last I heard. He's a great guy and I'm sure he'd be willing to help."

"I don't think I've met him."

"He's in another district, just east of Honey Ridge. I'll call tomorrow and leave a message at the phone shanty."

"What happens if Zach doesn't recover?"

"I know Zach; he can beat this. I think there's a battle going on in his head. While I stayed the night with him, he seemed to toss and turn all night. I think he might have been experiencing nightmares. He saw a lot of bad stuff out there in the world. Remember how he confessed that he'd killed several people when over in Afghanistan? Well, I think that might be coming back to haunt him."

"So, he wants to kill himself now?"

"No, I don't think so. I think he drinks to help him forget."

"But that's not going to help."

"I know. The folks he rents from are good people and they've been inviting him to their church. They have a program for people like Zach. I'm going to encourage him to go. Maybe I'll even go with him."

"You want to go to an *Englisch* church?" Her voice screeched.

"If it means getting help for Zach, then yes. You can go with us."

"*Nee.* I cannot do that. You shouldn't either. You know you'll be receiving a visit from the deacon if you keep this up."

"I'm sorry, but I don't know what else to do, Rosie.

I refuse to let Zach keep going down this destructive path that he's on. He has no one else to help him." He stroked her arm. "Let's not talk about this any more, okay? Let's talk about us."

"Us? There is no us, John. There's you and Zach. And then there's me. I feel like you're more committed to Zach than you are to our marriage."

Was that true? Had he neglected his wife that much? "I promise I'll make it up to you. When this is all over and straightened out, you'll see that it was just a short part of our lives. We can sacrifice a small amount of time to help a brother in need, *jah*?"

Chapter Seventeen

Glancing around his room for the night, which Frances informed him was once Rosanna's, Zach couldn't help but feel restless. It was all about to come back—the memories, the flashbacks, the nightmares. And this time he didn't have anything to dull the pain.

He sat on the bed and placed his head in his hands. John wanted to protect him from his addiction, protect him from the alcohol, but he didn't know that that wasn't what Zach feared. Drinking was only the symptom of his real problem. His counselor had called it PTSD—post-traumatic stress disorder—which basically meant the war haunted him.

John didn't understand the terrors that plagued Zach at every waking moment. The screams of his fellow soldiers, the ugly conditions, the blood everywhere. Nobody understood what he'd been through and no one would, unless they'd been through a similar ordeal.

He sighed and stood, pacing around the room. He did his best to step quietly, knowing most of the house was asleep. He resisted the pulls of slumber so they could sleep in peace. Zach knew if he were to sleep, his night terrors would surely awaken everyone. The only time he ever slept peacefully was when he drunk himself into unconsciousness.

Even now, being wide awake, the visions plagued him. He fought them as best as he could, tirelessly drawing his thoughts to other matters. He longed for the numbing oblivion that alcohol provided. It was his only escape from himself.

But, no matter how hard he tried, his mind always went back to that place, the hell that changed his life.

He reached for the camouflage backpack adjacent to his thigh.

"Take cover! Now!" his comrade yelled as he dived behind their temporary fortress.

Zach's gaze shot toward where Jones' voice announced the command. He glanced toward an abandoned building, spotted the enemy, and hastily crawled toward their makeshift sandbag wall, dragging his pack with him. A pop, pop, pop sound told him they were being fired upon.

He buried his head in the cocoon of his muscled biceps, compliments of growing up on an Amish farm, while sand flew from enemy fire. If only Bishop Hershberger could see me now. *He shook his head dispelling thoughts of home.*

Who knew if he'd even make it out of here alive? This was no time to lose his focus. There was a mission to accomplish—sneak in undetected, rescue the civilian refugees, and return home alive. But return to what?

Hadn't he sacrificed everything to come here? When he returned, there wouldn't be a parade in his honor like there would be for the other soldiers. There would be no loved ones with balloons or signs or welcoming him home. Stop it!

"Farm Boy? You okay?" Jones called.

Zach ignored his question. He listened in silence until fire from the enemy ceased. Rapid footsteps told him the enemy had moved on. Perhaps they hadn't been spotted after all. "Do you think they'll be back?"

"Most likely, but it looks like they've vacated the premises for now. I hear the Humvee coming." Jones crawled toward him. "Your leg looks like it's bleeding. Did you get hit?"

Zachariah looked down. Sure enough, there was a flow of crimson soaking the canvas pant leg at his ankle.

Jones cursed under his breath. "Quick, let's bind that up so you don't bleed to death."

To death? He certainly wasn't ready to die, not with the rift between him and the church.

"I'm fine. I didn't even feel anything." *Of course, after surviving a tractor accident, most pain never fazed him. He was no pansy.*

"Nevertheless, it's our job to look out for each other." Jones pushed Zach's pant leg up and winced. He pulled out a bandana from his pants pocket and wrapped it around his ankle tightly. "It looks pretty bad. One of the medics will have to treat it when we get back to the barracks. I don't have the proper supplies."

That was his fault. If they had stayed with the other

troops, none of this would have happened and they'd possess whatever supplies they needed. "Sorry, man."

"No time for apologies. Here comes Peters. Let's go." *Jones looked back at him.* "Here, put your arm around me. I don't think you can walk on that."

Zach stood up and attempted to put pressure on his wounded leg. Excruciating pain shot through his entire body and he thought he might pass out. He breathed heavily and quickly grasped on to Jones. "I don't know what I'd do without you. Thanks." *He forced the words through gritted teeth.*

Jones nodded with a frown. "You gonna be okay?"

"I think so." *A relieved sigh escaped Zach's lips as the convoy finally approached, but he didn't eagerly anticipate the tongue lashing he was sure to receive from his superior. It wouldn't be any worse than the bishop's rebuke, would it?*

Even so, he couldn't wait to get back home.

Jones' hand smacked his cheek, yanking him back to the present. "Don't you be falling asleep on me, Farm Boy. You can take your nap in the truck. Just a little further."

An explosion launched both men into the air. Zachariah's vision fuzzed, from the shock or the dust in his eyes, he wasn't sure. Return fire sounded from a few feet away, most likely their gunners. He spotted Jones lying face down beside him. "Jones?" *he managed, coughing at the dirt clinging to his tongue.*

Peters rushed to him. "Farm Boy! Can you walk?"

"Jones. Check Jones."

Peters rolled Zach's partner over then turned back to Zach, his face grim. "There's nothing we can do for him."

"Jones!"

"Come on, Farm Boy. You're first." Peters gripped
his arm and yanked him up. Zach screamed at the pressure on his wounded leg, torn open again from the re-
cent blast, while Peters hustled him to the vehicle. *"Get
him in,"* he commanded the soldiers, who hauled him
up into the back of the medic's truck.

Jones' still body landed next to him a few moments
later. Zach clenched a handful of his comrade's uni-
form and pulled him closer, trying to see his face. Sobs
choked him when he took in Jones' injuries. His face
and chest were torn open, revealing gaping flesh. The
right side of his face was mostly missing, leaving an
unrecognizable mess of blood.

Jones died saving my life. This is my fault.

*Unable to look into the face of his friend again, Zach
rested his head on Jones' limp arm and cried. "I'm
sorry. I'm so sorry. I'm so sorry."*

Zach pressed his hands over his mouth to stop his
screams from erupting. Silent tears coursed down his
cheeks. "I'm so sorry, Jones. I'm so sorry."

Leaning his forehead on his drawn-up knees, he
whispered those words over and over again, praying
that someday he might be able to redeem his mistakes.

"What do you do for a living, John?"

John stared out the window. Had he not even heard
her uncle's question? Rosanna nudged her husband.

"I'm sorry, what was that?" John shook his head.

"He asked about your job." "Frustrated" couldn't
begin to describe how Rosanna felt. Here they were,

at her relatives' place in Southern Ohio, on their honeymoon, and all he could think about was Zachariah Zook. This was supposed to be a time of bonding, but instead, it was driving a wedge further between them. She'd thought that if she just got John away from Kentucky, she'd have him all to herself. But, no. Zachariah was present wherever they went.

"Do you have a phone shanty?" John asked.

"Just down the road past the neighbor's house on the right." Her uncle pointed.

"Thank you." John pushed his chair back and headed in that direction. "I'll be back."

Rosanna's jaw dropped. She pushed her chair back too and followed after her husband. Once they were outside, she stopped him.

"John, please." She couldn't stop the tears that surfaced. "We haven't even been married a week and I already feel like I'm losing you."

He turned to her. "You're not. I'm still here and I'm not going anywhere."

"You may be here in body, but your mind is with Zachariah."

"I'm concerned about him, Rosie. Surely you can understand that." He leaned close and kissed her cheek. "I love you, Rosanna Christner."

"I wish you loved me more than Zach."

"That's ridiculous, Rosie. I didn't marry Zach, I married you." He tilted her chin toward him.

"It doesn't seem that way."

John's eyes met hers. "*Greater love hath no man*

than this, that a man lay down his life for his friends. Rosanna, do you believe the words of Jesus?"

"Yes, of course."

"I believe in living them. How else can we show love to one another? If I won't be Zach's friend, then please tell me, who will?"

How is it that the thing she loved about John was also the thing she hated? His kindness was one of the things that made her fall in love with him. Was *she* being the cruel one?

"So, you're willing to sacrifice me to take care of Zach? Is that it?"

"Rosie, listen to me. If we can help Zach, he will come back to us. Isn't that what we want? Isn't that the goal? How can loving someone and wanting what's best for them be a sacrifice? Can't we set aside our own needs for just a little bit? Think about it, Rosie. If Zach can get better, it will benefit the entire community. How happy would his folks be if he returned?

"What about the parables Jesus told? The lost coin. The lost sheep. We are supposed to go and look for the lost sheep just like the Good Shepherd would. We are not supposed to just leave him out there for the wolves to devour."

The sincerity in John's voice touched her heart.

Rosanna sighed. Perhaps *she* was the one being selfish. But was it really too much to desire her husband's attention? She realized that there was only one thing that could change their situation, and that was prayer. She would pray for her and John's marriage to not only succeed, but to thrive.

Chapter Eighteen

Zachariah had begun drinking again, and as a result, John and Rosanna returned from their honeymoon earlier than expected. They'd been blessed to receive nice gifts and Rosanna was happy that their families had shown much generosity toward them.

Upon finding out about Zach's departure and his drinking, John had been devastated. He blamed himself for being gone. Perhaps they should have postponed their trip like John had suggested in the first place, but how was Rosanna supposed to foresee the turn of events?

John apologized and rushed off as soon as they'd returned.

"Thanks, Ernie. I'll call you if I need a ride home later." John waved as the *Englisch* driver drove away.

He was visiting Zach again. He'd heard that his friend had taken to drinking again when he learned that another friend died in combat. Tommy had been the one to offer Zach a place to stay, so losing him must've really hit home. John knew he had a lot of work to do to pull Zach out of the pit he'd fallen into, but he was determined to do it, for good this time. It was his duty.

A middle-aged woman stepped out of the main house before he reached the door to Zach's apartment. "Excuse me? John, is it?"

"Yes, ma'am. It is. I'm a friend of Zach's."

"I'm Betty Brooks, his landlady. I was hoping we could talk for a moment."

"Of course."

"I've noticed that you've visited Zach several times and I'm assuming you are trying to help him recover from the war."

John nodded. "I am."

Mrs. Brooks smiled. "Good. I'm very glad he has a friend willing to help him. I've invited Zach to attend church with my husband and I. I'm sure it would help him. Our church provides a Reformers Unanimous program, which is designed to help people overcome their addictions."

Hope stirred within John. "I've been praying I could find something like that. What is the name of your church?"

"It's Crossroads Baptist. Just down the road a few miles. The RU meetings are at seven o'clock on Friday nights. I'm sure it would help him if he were to go."

"Thank you very much, Mrs. Brooks. And I will pray for the Lord to help you cope with the loss of Tommy."

Tears gleamed in her eyes. "Thank you, John. You

are a very kind young man. God bless you." The woman made her way back to the house.

John paused before opening Zach's door. *Lord, give me courage and perseverance. Help me bring Zach back to us. Heal his heart and soul. And please forgive me for my part.*

"As a leader and as one who cares for you, I advise you to steer clear of Zachariah Zook. He has left the ways of our people. Surely he is spreading a net out for your feet. Don't get entangled with him. It will only lead to heartache."

John stared at Deacon Miller. "I don't intend to leave, if that's what you're thinking."

"John, there have been many who have left who never *intended* to. That is how the devil works. He traps you until you have no way out. Most don't realize it until it's too late."

"Do you not think that Christ would try to help Zach-ariah?"

"Aye, but you are not Christ. You do not possess the fortitude to withstand the wiles of the devil."

"I'm glad to hear of your confidence in me."

"My confidence rests in Christ alone."

"As does mine."

"John, Bishop Hershberger asked me to speak with you on this matter. Surely, you would not wish to go against his...recommendations." His brow shot up at the implication the statement held. If he continued to associate with Zach, they would possibly put him under the *Bann* as well.

* * *

"I'll be back in a while." John's eyes met hers as he lifted his hat from the wall rack.

He already knew how she felt about this, so why was he still going? "But, John. You can't keep spending time with Zach. He's shunned."

"He's my friend, Rosanna. My best friend, in fact. He needs me. He needs my help now more than ever."

"The leaders are going to put *you* in the *Bann* if you continue to spend time with him. I don't want you to be shunned. You know how difficult that will make our lives." Could he hear the desperation in her voice?

"I can't help it, Rosie. I need to be there for him. You don't know what he's been through."

"But it's his own fault!"

John held up a hand to silence her, and Rosanna sensed a frustration in him that she'd never seen before. "Don't say that. I don't ever want to hear you say that again. He fought for this country. *Our* country. He fought to preserve our rights. Even if you don't agree with it, I won't have you blaming Zach. He did something more honorable than most people will ever do in their lifetime. He deserves respect."

"I don't understand how taking up a gun and shooting someone down is honorable," Rosanna reasoned.

"Just stop. Please." He stepped forward and placed a kiss on her forehead. "I love you, Rosie. You may not understand now, but I pray that someday you might. I have to go."

Animosity toward Zach grew in Rosanna's heart now more than ever. It wasn't enough that he had to leave the community and shame his family by joining the military, now he was destroying her and John's chance at a happy life. A tear slid down Rosanna's cheek as the back door slammed shut.

"So, Rosie, how have you and John been?" Margaret asked.

Rosanna glanced up from her stitching to meet her sister's gaze. She attempted to dispel the memories of their last fight from her mind. "Fine. Fine. Why do you ask?"

"Well…" her sister hesitated. "Seth mentioned that he saw him in town with Zachariah Zook a few days ago."

Rosanna blew out a breath and nodded.

"You knew?"

"Yes."

"I thought Deacon Miller warned him not to be around Zach," Frances entered the conversation from her side of the quilt.

Rosanna pretended to study her work, avoiding her mother and sisters' inquisitive gazes. "He did."

"Rosanna, if John is not adhering to the minister's instruction…" Her mother said gently.

"I know, *Mamm*. I know. I've spoken with him about it, but he insists he is doing what is right. He won't give up on Zach." She stabbed her needle into the quilt square, battling her anger—and her tears.

"Even if it costs him his family? His standing in the community? If he refuses to obey the leaders, he will be disciplined. This is very serious. You must convince him to stop his foolishness."

Frustration with John mounted. "I've tried, *Mamm*. I am trying. He's not listening. He is so determined that he is right. I just—I don't know what to do." She continued to watch her hands, which had ceased sewing and now lay useless.

Her mother's hand covered hers. "You will always have a home with us, Rosanna. If John continues to ignore the rules, he will be put under the *Bann*. If such a thing were to happen, your father and I will take you in. Don't ever doubt it."

"I won't, *Mamm*." Feeling the tears spill from her eyes, Rosanna stood. "I have to go."

Chapter Nineteen

Rosanna grinned in excitement as John's buggy pulled up beside the barn. He would come inside, greet her with a kiss, and then wash up for supper. Then after supper, and after the dishes were finished, they would both retire to the living room, where she would deliver her special news—if she could manage to wait that long.

She prayed this revelation would bring them closer together. The tension between them concerning Zach seemed to be straining their relationship, but hopefully that would all change now.

John's stomping footsteps could be heard from the back door as he entered the *dawdi haus*. He graced her with a warm smile. "How is my Rosie? Do you feel better this morning?"

She nodded. "I feel *wunderbaar*." Rosanna pressed her hands to his chest as she rose up on her tiptoes to kiss him, knowing how he loved it when she initiated the kiss.

"And so do I," John replied once their lips separated. "Especially now."

A grin crept up her mouth and she tapped his chest before stepping back. "Supper will be ready in a moment."

"I'll go wash up."

As John headed for the sink, she returned to the stove and transferred the food to the table. After quickly setting the table, they both bowed their heads in silent prayer. *Please be with the baby and protect it. And please heal the distance between John and I.* John cleared his throat to signal the end of the prayer and they both lifted their heads.

"How is the house coming along?" Rosanna asked.

"Good. I pray we'll be living in it by December." They shared a smile. There was something intimate about soon having a house they owned all to themselves.

"The sooner the better."

Rosanna dished out the chicken pot pie she'd made onto their plates so they could begin eating.

"Elam Zook visited me today."

She glanced up in question, unsure who that was.

"He's Zach's older cousin. He was at our wedding."

She nodded and a knot began forming in her stomach, as it always did when he brought up Zach.

"He said he wants to help me with Zach. He saw what happened at our wedding and he would like to help bring Zach back. I can't tell you how happy I am that someone else is on my side."

Rosanna glanced down at her food, the excitement in John's voice making her feel guilty. She knew she wasn't supporting him as a wife should, but how could she support him when she wasn't certain he was right?

John's hand covered hers. "I feel as though you're pulling away from me, Rosie. Please don't ever pull away from me."

She met his sober gaze and shook her head. "I'm not. I just hoped we could share an evening without discussing Zach."

"We can. And we will. I won't mention him any more today. I promise." He pressed a hand to his heart and raised the other in the air. His eyes twinkled.

Rosanna fought a grin at his foolishness.

"Come on, Rosie. Laugh. I'm funny and you know it." He wiggled his eyebrows and she giggled. "There it is. Have I ever told you I love to hear you laugh?" He caressed her cheek.

She leaned toward him. "I don't think so."

"Well, I do," he murmured, brushing her lips with a kiss.

The desire to share her news with John welled. She'd planned to wait until after supper, but now felt right.

"John," she began, his name interrupting their kiss.

He pulled back to meet her gaze, his hand still pressed to her cheek. "Yes?"

"I have something I need to tell you."

His brow furrowed at her serious tone. "What is it, *Schatzi*?"

She grinned. "I'm in the family way!"

John's countenance lit like a child at Christmas. "You are? Al—Already? You're sure?"

She nodded, joy filling her heart at her husband's excitement.

"Why didn't you tell me? How long—Is that why you felt sick the other day?"

She simply nodded again, struggling not to release her laughter.

"But, when did you find out?"

"Today. I thought I was but I took one of those *Englischer* pregnancy tests to be certain."

"Why didn't you tell me right away? I had no clue all this time and—" He shook his head. "What am I thinking? Who cares! I'm a *daed*!" He stood and pulled Rosanna to her feet. Gripping her waist, he stepped away from the table and swung her around. She laughed aloud, doubting she had ever been happier than she was in this moment. Suddenly, John stopped. "Wait, I probably shouldn't have done that. Is it bad for the *boppli*? I don't want to do anything to hurt it."

Rosanna laughed again. "I think the *boppli* is enjoying your excitement just as much as I am."

Wearing the biggest grin, John stepped close and branded his mouth to hers. Rosanna allowed her hands to travel up around his neck and lost herself in her husband's embrace. Some moments later, she looked up and noticed that she was in John's lap, sitting in the living room.

"Supper."

John removed her prayer kapp and began pulling out the pins securing her hair. He smiled. "Supper can wait."

Rosanna couldn't agree more.

Chapter Twenty

John leaned in and listened intently as the preacher spoke. He'd never understood the Scriptures as he had today. It was plain and clear. Jesus paid it all. *All*! There was nothing *anyone* could do to add to what Jesus did on the cross. Now, he knew what Jesus meant when he'd said, "It is finished."

This was absolutely amazing. If what the preacher read was true, that meant that there was nothing left to do. If you accepted Christ's sacrifice on the cross, your salvation was paid in full.

As this new revelation moved his heart, tears pricked his eyes. Every single one of his sins, past, present, and future, had been paid for by Jesus when He shed His blood.

He glanced toward Zach and hoped he'd been paying attention. The preacher asked if anyone wanted to receive Christ's free gift of salvation and John immediately threw his hand in the air. There was no way he was going to miss out on this opportunity.

After the service, the preacher approached him and asked if he'd like to talk more. You bet he did. He invited Zach to stay and listen, but he chose to wait with the Brooks family. They discussed several different things in regard to the message and John was happy to gain even more understanding. The Bible was clear. You could *know* that you were saved and Heaven bound!

John felt as though a heavy weight had lifted from his chest. He was free indeed! If only Zach could get a hold of this truth, how different his life would be.

He ached to get home so he could share his newfound knowledge with Rosie.

Rosanna smiled as John approached the house alone. She watched and sighed in relief as the taillights of Zach's vehicle rounded the corner. They would have the afternoon all to themselves—that is, if no one from their community showed up to visit, which was very likely on a Sunday.

"How's my beautiful wife?" He greeted her with a much needed kiss.

"*Gut*. How was your morning?" She moved to the dining area. "Are you hungry?"

"Not yet." He took her by the hand and led her into their sitting room. "Come, sit with me and let's talk." He sank down onto the couch and pulled her into his lap.

She loved the feeling of his arms around her waist. "About what?"

"I want to tell you what happened today."

He seemed so happy and Rosanna could almost feel his excitement. "Zach did what?"

"No, not Zach. This has nothing to do with Zach. It has to do with Jesus."

"Jesus?" Now she was a little confused.

"I got saved today, Rosie!" He squeezed her momentarily.

She wanted to catch his enthusiasm, but what did he mean by this? "I don't understand."

"Jesus paid it all."

Her brow rose. "Jesus paid it all?"

"Yes! When Jesus died on the cross for our sins, He paid for every one of them. Salvation is a gift and it's free for the asking." A grin stretched across his face and joy radiated from his eyes. "I asked Jesus to save me and I know He did! I'm going to Heaven, Rosie!"

"Why are you telling me this?"

He frowned. "Why am I telling you? I thought that was obvious."

A knock on the door interrupted their conversation. She sprung from his lap. It wouldn't do to be caught in an intimate embrace.

"Someone is here." She frowned and prayed it wasn't Zachariah Zook.

"I'll get it."

He pulled open the door and greeted their guests. "Isaac, Mary, it's *gut* to see you."

"*Mamm, Dat*, I didn't know you were coming by today." She smiled, relieved it wasn't Zach.

"We wanted to surprise you. I brought a casserole for supper."

John smiled. "That's *wunderbaar.*"

He leaned over and whispered in Rosanna's ear as

they took the dish to the kitchen. "Do you want to tell your folks about the *boppli*?"

She smiled and turned to her parents. "We have a surprise for you too!"

"Oh? Did you make my favorite dessert?" Her father perked up.

"No, *Dat*." She laughed.

"Rosie's in the family way!" John beamed.

"*Ach*, for real?" Her mother's countenance brightened. "Now, that's the best news I've heard in a long time!"

They shared congratulatory hugs.

"That was delicious, Mary. *Denki* for bringing it to us." John smiled at his mother-in-law.

Rosie's mother nodded demurely.

Rosanna's head shot up. "Did I hear something?"

"It sounded like a car." John moved to the door. *What's Zach doing back here?* He looked to the table, where Isaac still sat eating. The ladies had begun to take dishes from the table.

He quickly went outside before Zach could come in. The last thing he wished to do was disrupt a perfectly good evening with his wife and her parents.

"What's going on, Zach?" He met his friend as he opened his vehicle's door.

A whiff of his breath told him Zach had been drinking again. "Wanted to come see my buddy."

"Zach, you are not supposed to be driving while you're drinking, remember? If you drink, you need to stay home." Telling him now, while he was intoxicated, was as useful as telling an elephant to tie her shoes. "Get in the passenger's seat."

Zach did as told.

"Okay, now just wait there. I need to go talk to Rosie." He took the keys to ensure Zach wouldn't drive off.

He went to the door and called to Rosie. He quickly pulled her outside and closed the door. "I need to take Zach home. He's been drinking."

Rosie sighed and then nodded. "Okay. Are you going to call Ernie?"

"*Nee*, I'll just take him."

Her eyes sprang open. "But you don't drive."

"I did some driving when I was in my *rumspringa*."

"You did?" She smiled at this new revelation. "You never told me."

He shrugged. "It never came up."

"You're sure?"

"Yeah, it's no problem. And I'm going to ask Mrs. Brooks to hold onto his keys from now on so he can't drive drunk."

"That sounds like a *gut* idea."

He pulled his wife close and gave her a kiss she wouldn't forget too soon. "I love you, Rosanna Christner."

"I love you, too. Please don't be any longer than you have to."

"I won't." He pointed to the house. "Do you want me to explain to your folks?"

"*Nee*. I can handle it. You go." She put a hand against his chest and kissed him, sending a spark of desire through his veins. "The sooner you leave, the sooner you'll be back." Her lips met his one more time before she disappeared into the house.

Boy, did he love his wife! His blessings almost seemed too much to contain.

Now, if he could just get Zach back on his feet again, the world would be right.

"Let's get you home, buddy." He turned the engine over and pulled out of the driveway.

Chapter Twenty-One

A knock on the door woke Rosanna from a dead sleep. She rubbed her eyes, loathing the fact that she needed to answer the door. Who could it be? She knew it wasn't John, he wouldn't knock. She rolled over and looked at the empty spot in bed next to her—an all too common sight since their wedding a few months ago. She'd hoped that telling John about the baby the other night would influence his decision to be home early in the evenings. It hadn't. She sighed, put her robe on, and went to open the door.

"Who is it?" She called through the door before opening it.

"It's Henry Christner."

John's father? What was he doing here at this hour?

She quickly opened the door and her eyes widened when she noted the police officer behind him.

"Rosanna," Henry swallowed and she noticed tears in his eyes. "There's been an accident."

"An accident?" Her gaze shot from John's father to the officer.

"John is dead."

Rosanna felt her knees go weak.

"Is she dead?" Rosanna heard her father-in-law say.

"No, she just passed out." *Whose voice was that?* It was unfamiliar.

She felt cool air on her face and she opened her eyes. Was she lying on the floor? "What happened?" She looked to her mother, then to John's father, then to an officer. What was going on?

"You fainted," her mother explained.

Fainted? She'd never fainted before. "Why?"

"You do not remember?" John's father asked. His eyes shifted to the officer.

"*Nee.*" She looked around. "Where's John?"

Her mother stroked her hair. "He's gone."

"*Jah, jah.* With Zachariah." She sat up slowly. Her memory was returning now.

"No, *dochder.* John was in a car accident with Zachariah Zook. He is dead."

She closed her eyes and attempted to process her mother's words. "Zachariah is dead?"

"*Nee*, our John is dead." Henry Christner's brow lowered.

"John? *M—my* John?" Her hand immediately went to her belly. No, John couldn't be dead. He couldn't be! He had to be here to help her raise their baby. She couldn't raise it alone. "No! He can't be dead!"

"I'm very sorry, ma'am," the officer spoke. "Is there something we can do for you?"

"*Nee*, you may go now," Henry Christner nodded to the officer.

"I will stay here with her, Henry. You may go home to your family," her mother said. "But will you help me get her to the chair?"

"Sure," Henry said.

"I can do it. I don't need help," Rosanna insisted. She attempted to stand but her legs gave way again. Her mother and Henry caught her by the arms.

"Let us help you, *dochder*," her mom said. She and Henry helped her over to the chair in their small gathering room.

"You wanna help me? Bring John back." Tears rushed to the surface and cascaded down her cheeks. "I can't live without him."

Her mother pulled her close and let her cry on her shoulder. "I know it is hard, *dochder*. But *Der Herr* will be with you. He will help you through this."

"I'm not ready to let him go, *Mamm*. Our *boppli*…" She couldn't speak another word as the tears choked her voice. Her heart felt like it had been wrung out like a rag. Not a drop of anything was left. It ached more than she could fathom.

"Shh…" Her mother continued stroking her hair, but it didn't lessen the pain.

If only she could die too. If only she didn't have to face her future alone.

John's body was delivered to his parents the next morning. Sarah Christner prepared his body and dressed him in the clothing he wore on the day of his and Rosanna's wedding. Family and friends visited to view the body and offer condolences. Rosanna stayed home, unable to shake the shock clouding her mind. She knew many of the Amish would question her absence, but she paid it no thought. John was gone.

Sleep refused her that night and she spent the hours gazing upon the empty space beside her. It seemed as though all she could do was think about their last hours together. The pride of informing her parents of their new *boppli*. The disappointment in letting him leave with Zach. The sorrow and pain she experienced when she learned he was gone. The memories replayed over and over again, and yet the tears never came.

The funeral arrived too soon the following day and Rosanna forced herself to rise and join her parents and sisters on their way to John's childhood home. The sight of the special buggy created to carry coffins parked by the barn seemed to make everything seem so real. Her mother guided her inside the house and to John's *mamm*.

Sarah's eyes brightened with tears. "I will take you to see him."

Rosanna reluctantly followed the woman into a room, where an open coffin was supported by two church benches. Her feet drew her nearer to her husband's life-less body. As she gazed upon the pale, still face that was once her precious John, acid rose in her throat and she turned and rushed out of the room and through the back door. She retched onto the ground, tears blinding her vision. "Why, *Gott*? Why?" Sobs choked her and she didn't fight them. "Why did it have to be John? Why my John?"

How long she sat there crying, she didn't know. Somehow, releasing her pent-up tears seemed to cleanse her. It didn't take away the pain, the horror, but it brought some solace. The wall had finally crumbled and she mourned for what she had lost. Who she and her baby had lost. She wept until her head ached nearly as much as her heart.

Suddenly, she noticed her *mamm*'s hand on her shoulder. "Rosanna. We need to go now. The funeral is about to begin."

She nodded and rose to her feet, wiping her face with her handkerchief. Praying for strength, she entered the room where the funeral was to be held and was surprised to see how many folks had arrived. She sat in her designated place, grateful that she was unable to see the body from her view.

The first minister selected to speak soon began. "John Christner was born to Henry and Sarah Christner twenty-two years ago. He…"

The preacher spoke about John, outlining his childhood and adult life, and discussing his good standing in the church and community. Rosanna listened to the familiar stories, her mind refusing to focus on anything, until the minister's words grabbed her attention.

"John was living in sin the last weeks of his life. He chose to openly fellowship with a shunned member of our community and ignored repeated warnings to cease his foolish actions. He brought shame upon his family."

The man's words felt like a dishonor to John, yet did she not agree with him? Wasn't she also against John's actions?

"And how did he die? He perished in an *Englisch* vehicle, while driving with an intoxicated shunned member."

The police officer's words came back to her. *"From what witnesses have said, your husband saw a deer in the road and swerved out of the way. He lost control of the vehicle and crashed into a tree. He most likely died upon impact."*

"We can only hope that John repented in his final moments and prayed for *Gott* to forgive him of his transgressions. Perhaps if he did so, his soul went to Heaven."

She recalled John's words on the night he died. *"I asked Jesus to save me and I know He did! I'm going to Heaven, Rosie!"*

Was John in Heaven? Was there a chance she could see him again? Rosanna prayed it was so. Her heart ached with the longing to see her husband again. Not his lifeless body, but the man she knew and loved. She yearned to kiss him one more time, to beg him to take her with him.

The service lasted another hour, but Rosanna didn't hear a word. When the funeral was over, the congregation rose and prepared their buggies for the drive to the cemetery. Rosie was heading for her parents' buggy when Magdalena approached her.

"Oh, Rosanna, I'm so sorry! I came as soon as I could." Her best friend's eyes filled with tears and Rosanna wrapped her arms around her, her own tears welling.

"Thank you for coming. I appreciate it."

They both rode with her parents and sisters to the Amish cemetery less than a mile away. John's casket was carried to the freshly dug grave and lowered into it. Sarah wept openly as the casket was slowly buried, until the entire hole was filled.

Wiping a tear, Rosanna glanced away and spotted a single figure standing just outside of the cemetery fence. Noticing her gaze, the person turned and limped away.

How dare Zachariah Zook come here! It was all his fault John was gone, all his fault she was widowed at eighteen, his fault her and John's *boppli* would grow up without its biological father.

And she certainly had a mind to tell him so.

Chapter Twenty-Two

Zachariah watched from afar as the long line of buggies drove toward the Amish cemetery and eventually parked near what would be John's final resting place. He couldn't help shedding tears as they laid to rest the best friend he'd ever had. Few people possessed the character and integrity of John Christner and it was unfortunate for those who knew and loved him that he had to leave this earth so early.

Nobody could possibly understand the ways of God, but Zach found it difficult not to question his Maker. Rosanna didn't deserve to have her husband taken from her so soon. John didn't deserve to die. As a matter of fact, he was less deserving than anyone he knew. But maybe God saw things differently. Heaven was a blessing, not a curse. Perhaps it was *because* John was such a great guy that God *rewarded* him with an early death.

Rosanna heard the footsteps, but she didn't turn at the sound of them. It wasn't John. It would never again be John's footsteps approaching. Oh, how she wished she could just disappear and cease to exist.

"Rosanna?" Magdalena's gentle voice called.

She looked up when she felt her friend's hand on her shoulder.

Magdalena sat down next to her on the couch—the couch where she had sat in John's lap just a few days ago. To be able to feel his arms around her just one more time!

"Can I help you with something? Would you like to talk?"

Her friend had always been thoughtful and kind. "*Nee*. Talking won't bring John back." Another avalanche of tears cascaded down her cheeks.

"No, it won't. But it might make you feel better."

"I don't see how that's possible." She pushed the wetness off her face. "He was just going to take Zach home. Not even twenty minutes away. I don't understand, Magdalena. Why didn't God direct the deer along another path? Why did it have to be in front of John? Why did Zachariah have to show up here drunk? We were having such a *gut* time here with my folks. We just told them about the *boppli*."

Magdalena's mouth draped open. "*Boppli*?"

"I maybe shouldn't have said anything."

Magdalena put a hand on her hip, feigning offense. "You intended to keep this secret from your best friend? Oh, Rosanna, I think that is wonderful that you are going to have a sweet little one to remember John by! You've been given a special gift." She chuckled. "And

I can't say I'm surprised by the way I saw you and John kissing that day."

Rosanna giggled just a little. It had been her first bit of happiness since hearing of John's death.

"See? Now that's how John would want you to be."

Rosanna nodded. "You're right. He loved making me laugh."

"Well, I think that whenever you feel down, you need to think of one of John's jokes."

"It's hard. You'll never know what a *gut, gut* man John was."

"No, but you do. And I'm glad that he left you with fond memories. You know, not everybody gets that blessing."

"Well, *jah*. But they're not all *gut* memories. I'd been frustrated with him a lot lately."

"Whatever for? You guys looked so happy at the wedding."

"Remember what happened at the wedding?"

"You mean the drunk *Englisch* guy who said he kissed you?

She nodded. "Yep, that'd be Zachariah Zook. He used to be Amish. And he was John's best friend."

"Oh."

"Zach left and became a soldier. He lost part of his leg. Anyway, he's been drinking a lot and John has been trying to help him stop. He hoped to bring him back to our people." Rosanna sighed.

"And that was a *bad* thing?"

"I don't know. Maybe I was just being selfish to want my husband home with me. I just felt like Zach was stealing him away from me. And it's true. Now John's gone and I'll never be able to look at his face again."

"I don't think it was selfish—of you or of John. I think you were just kind of caught in the middle of all of it. Of course John would want to help his best friend, right?"

"I suppose so."

"So, what's going to happen with Zach now that John's gone? Do you think his drinking will get worse?"

Honestly, she hadn't thought much about Zach in a compassionate way. She'd been so angry with him. She was still angry with him. "I don't know."

"Is he shunned?"

Why was Magdalena asking all these questions about Zach? She didn't want to think about him right now. She sighed. "Yes."

"So, he basically has nobody now that John's gone?"

"I—I don't know. I guess so."

"That's really sad. I hate to say it, but it wouldn't surprise me if his funeral isn't too far off."

Rosanna's jaw dropped.

"Think about it, Rosanna. He has no family or friends. He's injured from the war so he probably can't do too much. It's no wonder he's drinking."

Put that way, Rosanna felt ashamed. How was it that John and Magdalena could both see it, but she was blind to it? "But it's his own fault."

"For leaving, maybe. But how could he know that all this would happen?"

"I really *don't* want to talk about Zachariah Zook. I'm sorry, Magdalena."

"No, that's okay. We don't have to. Just think about it some."

Rosanna nodded.

"Well, I'm gonna go heat up some supper for us. We have all this delicious food here. You know, if you freeze some of it and take it out here and there, you'll probably be set for at least a month. Maybe I'll move in." She smiled.

"*Ach*, I would love that."

"Me, too. But I don't think *Mamm* and *Dat* will allow it." She stuck out a pouty lip. "They've already mentioned how worldly Honey Ridge is. You've got me for another week, though."

"I'm glad. You will be a big help to get my mind off John. *Denki* for being here for me."

"That's what *gut* friends are for. And when my future husband dies, I expect you to do the same." Magdalena laughed, despite the serious nature of her comment.

Rosanna shook her head, but breathed a prayer of thanksgiving for her friend.

Chapter Twenty-Three

Zach couldn't believe it. He'd been sober for three weeks now! It had been the three most excruciating weeks of his life, and not just because of the lack of alcohol. It was true that the alcohol had helped to dull some of the physical pain and temporarily forget his emotional struggles, but now he had another hardship piled onto his mountain of troubles. He'd lost one of the best gifts he'd ever been given—the gift of John's friendship. His inability to cope had cost him more than he cared to admit.

How could God take him from this world? Rosanna needed him. He needed him.

If only he could have gotten sober before John's death. If only they could have had a two-sided friendship his last remaining days on earth. But it was too late. John was dead, and it was entirely his fault. There was absolutely nothing he could do to bring him back. There was nothing he could do to make things right. He'd never be able to apologize. He'd never be able to thank his best friend for the selfless devotion he'd poured into their relationship.

Because of his alcohol dependency, Rosanna had lived alone most of her brief married life. He'd stolen the precious time she could have spent with her new husband. She hadn't even known about the activities he and John had been involved in. She hadn't known about John's conversion, unless he'd told her the day of his death, which was quite possible.

That was the only thing that now brought comfort to Zach's soul. He knew beyond the shadow of a doubt that John was in Heaven. And he knew that, because he too had accepted Christ just after John's death, he would see his best friend again someday. God was truly gracious.

Who knew that it would take John's death and his own conversion to cure his idiocy? God knew. Which now made him wonder, what did God have planned for his future?

Zachariah knew he was well on the way to recovery, and for that he was thankful. He currently met with the pastor twice a week and he'd been offering a lot of Godly counsel. He found that most of his inner spiritual turmoil had stemmed from false interpretation of certain passages of Scripture.

He desperately wanted to know what God said, especially in regard to non-resistance, a long-held belief of his Amish ancestors. They'd always taught that military service, or being a peace officer, went against Jesus' teachings on loving your enemies. Killing was wrong, no matter what.

"The Bible says, *Thou shalt not kill*," Zach reasoned with the pastor.

"I'd like to show you something, Zach." The pastor opened his Bible to the book of Matthew. "Do you remember the story of the young rich man that came to Jesus?"

"I think so. He went away sad because he had much worldly goods."

"That's right. But there's something else that struck me as interesting about that passage." He turned to chapter nineteen. "Remember when Jesus cited the Ten Commandments?"

Zach nodded.

"Jesus says something very interesting here, and I think a lot of people miss it. Let me read. *Jesus saith unto him, Thou shalt do no murder.*" He looked up at Zach. "Did you see that? Jesus defined for us what the commandment means."

"So, *thou shalt not kill* means *thou shalt not murder*?"

"Exactly. Look at this way, Zach. God's Word will never contradict itself when rightly divided. If we're confused on some point, I guarantee you we're reading it wrong. That's why we're exhorted to study God's Word." He turned to another passage. "Do you realize in Romans, the Bible calls those that bear the sword 'ministers' of God? Those that bear the sword would be police officers and soldiers. Imagine if only ungodly men held these positions. Do you think they would be protecting you?"

"I imagine not."

"Also, if you look in the book of Nehemiah, the people were commanded to *fight* to protect their families. I don't think God is against people protecting themselves. As a matter of fact, the Bible says that he that provideth not for his own is worse than an infidel. I would say that protection is a basic need. "Do you know what the Lord required of His people in the Old Testament?"

Zach shook his head.

"To do justly, to love mercy, and to walk humbly with their God. There is nothing just or merciful about letting an evil person slaughter your loved ones."

Hmm… Zach thought for a moment. *Then the story of Jacob* Hochstetler *is* wrong?

"It is true that Jesus said to love our enemies, and we should. We should love our neighbor and do good. But that doesn't abrogate the fact that we need someone to bear the sword, someone to execute justice. Officers of the law don't go around killing people, at least not without just cause. Their job is to keep the peace so that we can live without fear, so we can live in freedom."

Zach nodded. "Why does it seem so clear? And why do others not see these things?"

"Zach, I think a lot of times people approach the Bible with their own ideas. When they have their own ideas, they want to justify them. What each one of us should be doing is opening ourselves up to the truth, no matter if it challenges our thinking. Because, when it all comes down to it, it won't matter what you believe or what I believe. What matters is the truth. You can believe the sky is bright green if you want to and I can believe it's purple, but in reality it's blue. It's the same with religion. One person can believe in Buddha and another can believe in Muhammed, but God will always be God and Jesus will always be the only way to Heaven. One cannot change the truth by not believing it."

Wow! If only the Amish leaders would sit down and discuss the Scriptures with the pastor. But Zach knew the chances of that happening were nearly impossible.

Since Magdalena had returned to Indiana and the flow of visitors faded, Rosanna found that she had more and more time to herself. Time that she used to spend cleaning, gardening, and sewing, all the while dreaming of her husband and their bright future, was now spent sitting, rocking, crying, and thinking. Thinking about her poor babe, who would never know its *daed*. Thinking about John and the way things used to be. Thinking about Zachariah Zook, and how all of it was his fault.

Her anger was like a rock weighing on her chest and she longed to release it, to find the root of her trouble and unleash her emotion. She tried to think of her friend's words and feel sympathy for Zach, but if he was miserable, it was all his fault. No one forced him to leave their people and join the military. No one forced him to drink. No one forced him to ruin his life. In fact, the one person who'd tried to help him ended up suffering and being killed—all because of Zachariah Zook.

Rosanna knew the hate festering inside of her wouldn't help, but she was powerless to stop it. Just as she'd been powerless to keep John away from Zach.

When a knock shook her door that morning, she was tempted to pretend she wasn't home. She doubted she could feign a normal conversation right now. Wondering who would visit her when most Amish folks were busy at home working, she peeked out the window and frowned at the sight of an unfamiliar car. Who was it?

She reluctantly opened the door and froze.

"Hello, Rosanna." Zach's tone held caution. If he knew how she felt about him, it would hold fear too.

She didn't respond, didn't invite him in.

"I came to apologize…for everything I've done. I've been so selfish."

Still, she remained silent.

"May…may I come in?"

If her heart hadn't been so callous to him, she would have cried at the hesitance in Zach's once-confident voice.

Despite herself, she opened the door a bit wider, allowing him inside the house. She shut the door after him.

"I'm so sorry for your loss, Rosanna. Can you please forgive me?"

Her heart hardened at the tears in his eyes. There was no possible way he hurt as badly as she did. "How can I possibly forgive you when you took John from me? He was the only man I ever loved and he's gone. He's gone because of you. He'll never see his own *boppli* because of you."

"*Boppli*?" Zach's shoulders slumped further. "Rosanna, I had no idea. I'm so sorry. I wish I could help—"

Somehow, his sympathy made things worse. "You can't! There's nothing you can do to bring him back.

Why did he have to die? Why my husband? He was innocent. He didn't deserve to die." Tears stung her eyes and she was helpless to stop them. Just as she was helpless to stop the flow of words.

"I... I hate you, Zachariah Zook! And if I never see you again, it'll be too soon." Rosanna could no longer keep her emotions at bay. She was tired of holding all of her anguish inside. "If you hadn't gone into the military, none of this would have happened. You go off and leave all your family and friends to fight for something that we're against. You thought you'd come home as some sort of hero. Well, guess what? *You're* not the hero. You got injured and started drinking, and who tried to save you? John! *He* was the hero. And then you...you killed him!"

Zachariah hung his head and spoke softly. "If that's how you see it, then I suspect you'd never believe the truth anyway."

"The truth? What are you talking about?" She pushed away a frustrated tear.

Chapter Twenty-Four

He moved toward the door of Rosanna's home. His hand paused on the handle. *Why did I even come here?* "Just...never mind. Forget I said anything." Zach shook his head. "Goodbye, Rosanna."

"No. You will not leave like that! Tell me what you meant by what you just said," she insisted.

He sighed. He shouldn't have said anything. Rosanna wasn't ready to hear what he had to say. Right now, she wanted someone to blame for her grief. Though he couldn't fault her, he longed for her to know the truth. But should he really be telling her this? He had to. She had to know. "You really wanna know, huh? Well, this was all for you."

"What do you mean *for me*? Don't you dare go blaming your problems on me!"

"Incredible." He shook his head. She was too blinded by her emotions now. He should just leave.

"What do you mean by that?"

"Never mind. I shouldn't tell you. You wouldn't believe the truth anyway. Not coming from me." *Would she even care what the truth was?*

She swiped at a tear. "I want to know."

"I don't think you do." He turned to go.

A surprisingly firm grip on his arm stopped him. "Tell me what you have to say."

Slowly, he turned to face her. "Fine. I left because John didn't want to go. *He's* the one who signed up for it. He's the one who wanted to be a soldier."

Her brow wrinkled in confusion. "I don't understand."

"John was going to jump the fence. I thought he was crazy when he told me he'd joined the military. It was just before your family moved here. You know, our people have always been against war. He had every intention of becoming a soldier and most likely leaving the Amish. His folks didn't know. No one knew."

"I don't know if I can believe that."

Praying she would believe him, Zachariah continued, "He begged me to take his place after he met you. He must have fallen for you pretty hard. He didn't want to leave and ruin his chances with you. Remember the last night before I left? Our conversation on the porch? That's why I wanted to be sure that you weren't playing games."

Rosanna shook her head. "But why would you do that?"

"I really didn't want to, but I saw it as a way to keep my best friend here amongst our people. I just couldn't imagine him leaving and the heartbreak it would cause in the community. He'd found you. And that meant he'd probably get married and stay. You were the answer to my prayers.

"We've always been told we look so much alike that we could be brothers. When John got his driver's license, it was amazing how much his picture looked like me. He'd already completed all the paperwork and what not. All that was left to do was to report for duty. So, after John explained everything he knew about the military to me, I went in and took his place. We didn't even know if it would work. It was a shot in the dark, and if we were ever found out..." He sighed. "And the funny thing about it is, from the time I was in basic training to when I served in the Middle East, and my whole time in the military, I had to tell myself I was John Christner. The guys actually called me Farm Boy." He chuckled. "To this day, the government thinks I'm John Christner."

"But that's illegal, *ain't so*?"

"Probably could go to prison for it." He shrugged. "But it's true."

"*Prison*?" She shook her head and swallowed. "So, you were shunned in John's place?"

He grasped a clump of his hair. "Swear you won't tell a soul! I shouldn't even be telling you this. I *promised* John. I was supposed to take it to the grave. Nobody can ever know. Promise me, Rosanna, that you won't tell anyone. He never wanted you to know. He didn't want you to be disappointed in him."

"I won't swear, but I won't tell either."

He expelled a relieved breath.

"But I still don't understand. Why would you do that?"

He shrugged. "I loved John like a brother. And I know he would've done the same for me if I'd asked.

What if he'd gone off to war and gotten killed? I never would've been able to live with myself if that happened."

"But you could go to prison. You put yourself in harm's way. *You* could have been killed. You sacrificed your life and your family. And your leg. You'll never be able to walk like you used to."

"It doesn't matter."

"Of course it matters. Everything you've experienced is a result of your military service and leaving the Amish. Is that why John…" she let her voice trail off. She stared out into the field the window revealed. A tear slid down her cheek. "I, I don't know what to say."

Could you really like somebody and hate them at the same time? He was certain these were her feelings as this new information processed. "You don't have to say anything." He sighed.

"But I've treated you so wrongly. Here, I thought that you left us because you were a selfish jerk. I judged you harshly. I thought you had to prove something."

"I deserved it. And I'm sorry for causing John's death. I hope someday you can forgive me." He watched Rosanna for a moment, then turned to go. "And by the way, I thought you should know that I stopped drinking the day John died."

Zach was unsure what he was expecting to accomplish by telling Rosanna all this, but at least now she knew the truth and she could process it however she wanted to.

Chapter Twenty-Five

Rosanna stood dumbfounded. How could Zachariah's words be true?

She thought about her time with John and how he'd reacted to everything that had happened. No wonder he'd felt it was his duty to take care of Zach! He must've felt indebted to his best friend for his sacrifice. It was like he owed him a debt that could never be paid.

That explained his favorite Bible verse, "*Greater love hath no man than this, that a man lay down his life for his friends.*" He hadn't been using it in reference to himself, all this time he'd been thinking about Zach.

Now it all made perfect sense.

The more she understood, the more the ice around her heart thawed. She had been so wrong. Zachariah Zook wasn't anything like she thought him to be.

The day John asked Zachariah to stand in his stead seemed like just yesterday. He'd been hesitant when John handed him the envelope with all his information.

He'd already known that John had a driver's license and had taken the test for his GED, but he had no idea that he also owned a Social Security card and had an actual birth certificate. He'd wondered just how long John had been preparing for his venture into the military. And had he acquired all this information without his folks' knowledge? How on earth had he kept it all a secret? Of course, Zach was the only one who knew John was thinking of leaving the Amish. That was the main reason he'd agreed to the whole military thing. If John and Rosanna married, John would remain Amish his entire life. Never in his imagination had he thought that *he'd* be the one to leave the Amish. Nor had he thought his best friend's life would be cut so short.

If it weren't for Jesus, it would have all been in vain.

Zachariah hobbled to the door. It wasn't often he received visitors, especially since John had been gone. The wound of knowing he'd been partially responsible for his best friend's death seemed to tear open daily. But now, instead of turning to alcohol for comfort, he'd been turning to God's Word.

He knew that to desire John's widow's forgiveness had been an unreasonable expectation. He had hoped that after he explained the truth, she would be a little more sympathetic to his plight. But, after an entire week with nary a word from her, it seemed it wasn't meant to be.

He pulled the door open. "Rosanna? What are you doing here?"

"I'm hoping you'll take John's place again."

He blinked. "What do you mean?"

"I've been thinking and praying about it a lot since we talked. This *boppli* is going to need a *gut vatter* and I can't think of anyone I'd rather have as a husband."

"Whoa! What a minute. Are—Are you proposing to me?" He swallowed.

She shrugged. "If that's what you want to call it."

"But, I don't understand. You said you hated me. You never wanted to see me again. Why would you ask me to marry you?" Zach was having trouble wrapping his head around the idea. Rosanna had never liked him. Even when they'd first met, she'd been attracted to him, but he doubted she ever harbored any true feelings for him. He, on the other hand, hadn't been able to stop caring for her. But now that the moment he dreamed of was here, he was hesitant to hope she felt the same way he did.

She bowed her head a moment before meeting his eyes. Tears glistened. "I've been a fool. All this time I've despised you for leaving your family and your best friend. I never realized that they were the reason you left. That your sacrifice was for them. For me."

He looked away, uncomfortable at the praise she was pinning on him. "I ruined your life, Rosanna. John—"

"Shh." Her finger flew to his lips to silence him. "Because of your sacrifice, I experienced some of the best months of my life with John. And who knows what would have happened if *he* was the one that had gone into the military? Who knows if we would have ever married or if he would have even survived? Don't you see? You saved him, Zach. I could never thank you enough for that.

"At first, I didn't want to believe you when you told me the truth. I harbored bitterness toward you, Zach. I didn't want to think that *you* had been the noble one, and that I had been wrong. But I was wrong and denying it couldn't change that. And now I know that you weren't the man I assumed you to be. In fact, you're so much better. And there's nothing I would rather do than spend the rest of my life with that man."

She touched his cheek. "And the truth is, I was attracted to you from the very beginning. I know if John hadn't captured my heart, I most likely would have fallen in love with you. And now, I believe I have. God has blessed me by letting me love two of the best men on this earth."

Her revelation was overwhelming. Could he truly allow himself to believe it?

"I don't know, Rosanna. I could never fill John's shoes."

"I don't believe that. Besides, I don't *want* you to be John. I want you to be *you*. You see, I've fallen in love with *you*, Zachariah Zook. *You* have been the selfless one in this equation. You are the one who sacrificed everything so John and I could have a future. And I can't imagine a life without you here."

Her comforting words warmed his soul like a blazing fire on a wintry morning. But, as much as he longed to, he knew he couldn't simply accept. So many things had changed. "You know what you're asking of me, right? You're asking me to go back to my family and community and make a kneeling confession. You're asking me to become Amish again."

She nodded.

"I don't know, Rosanna. My beliefs have changed. I'm not sure if I can abide by the *Ordnung*."

"What do you mean?"

Lord, please speak to Rosanna's heart. "When I left the Amish, I met someone who told me about Jesus."

"But didn't you already know about Jesus? I don't understand."

"It's not enough to know *about* Jesus. We need to have a personal relationship with Him."

Rosanna frowned. She tried to recall what John had told her about Jesus before he died.

Zach grabbed His old Bible from the coffee table. "Do you know what this is?"

"*Die Heilige Schrift*?"

"That's correct. It's a German Bible. Have you read it?"

"Some."

"And what did you think of what you read from it?"

Rosanna shrugged. "I didn't really understand much of it."

"Why would God give us a book we can't understand?"

"I don't know. But the ministers and the bishop know what it says. That's why we go to meeting on Sunday."

"That's not good enough for me, Rosanna. See, I think God desires that every person know Him. I think that He wants us to read the Bible and understand it for ourselves, not just believe every word the ministers speak."

"But how can we understand it ourselves?"

Zach put the German Bible back on the table and took his English Bible in his hands. "Let me read something to you." He flipped the pages to a passage in First John and read, "*He that hath the Son hath life; and he that hath not the Son of God hath not life.*" He looked at her. "Do you understand that verse?"

"I think so. It said that if a person has the Son then they have life. And the person that doesn't have God's Son doesn't have life."

"That's right. And if we keep reading, the next verse explains that the 'life' that is written about is 'eternal life.' You see, it's not really that difficult to understand, is it?"

She shook her head.

"Rosanna, do *you* have the Son of God? I know that you've heard about Him." He pointed to the verse. "This doesn't say if you've heard about Jesus then you will have eternal life, it says that if you *have* God's Son."

"How can I *have* God's Son? I don't know what that means."

He handed her his Bible. "Here, read the next verse. One thing I've learned about the Bible is that if you read all the verses in the context, you will be able to understand it much better." *Help her to understand, Lord. Help her to believe in You.*

"Okay." Rosanna took his Bible and read the words silently. She looked up at him. "So, the word *believe* is to *have* Jesus? Believe what?"

"Let's read John chapter three. I think it will give you a clearer understanding of what it means to believe." He turned to the passage and handed her the Bible.

He continued, "But, basically, if you believe that Jesus Christ died for *your* sins and you accept His payment for them, you will be saved. See, we all have sin. Sin blocks our way to Heaven. It's impossible to remove our sin on our own. God knows that and that's why He sent Jesus. A perfect blood sacrifice is required for the payment of sin. Jesus was the only one who's ever lived that could pay for sins. I can't pay for your sins because I'm not perfect—only Jesus is."

Rosanna nodded in understanding.

"So, when we give our sins to Jesus to pay for, it's like He gives us a brand new white robe to wear and this robe is made of His righteousness. So, when God looks at us, He no longer sees our sin because our sin is no longer there. All God sees is the righteousness of His Son. It is a gift that cannot be earned, it can only be received. And *this* is what is required to enter Heaven." He looked into her eyes. "Does this make sense to you?"

She lifted a half-smile. "I think so."

"Well, I don't want you to take my word for any of it. I want you to read it for yourself." Zach got up and went to his bedroom while Rosanna read over John three. He returned with a thin brown book. "Here, I want you to have this."

"What is it?"

"It's the Gospel of John in English, German, and Pennsylvania Dutch."

She took the book from his hand. "Really? I didn't even know they made such a thing."

"Take it home with you. Read it so you can understand for yourself. When I have a chance, I'll get you an English Bible."

"*Denki.*" She set the book down next to her. "I didn't really expect to come over here and read the Bible."

"I never expected it either."

"What did you think of my question?" She whispered.

His brow arched. "The proposal?"

"*Jah.*"

"Well, I think I need to pray about it. A lot." He sighed, knowing that, despite their newfound love, whichever road they took would be difficult. "Don't get me wrong, Rosanna. There's not much in this life I'd love to have more than you as my wife and the privilege of raising John's only child. I love you. I think I always have." He resisted the desire to touch her, kiss her. "But I don't know how we can get around the Amish church. You're a good-standing member. I, on the other hand, am shunned. And I know that they would accept me back into the church if I made a kneeling confession. But how can I agree to something I don't agree with? I would be living a lie."

"What don't you agree with?"

"Well, first and foremost, salvation. Those verses we read in First John clearly say one can be saved and know that they have eternal life. Second, is the belief that those who leave the Amish are doomed to certain Hell. There are many Amish who have left and have trusted Christ as their Saviour. The Bible clearly states they will not go to Hell. On the contrary, anyone— Amish or not—who rejects Jesus' payment for their sin, is subject to condemnation. You can read that in John three, thirty-six. You see, things the Bible states plain as day are rejected by our leaders. I don't understand it."

"Do you think that maybe they have not read these verses?"

"I think that the teachings of the Amish church are so engraved in the leaders' minds because they have been passed down for so many generations. They hold those teachings sacred, no matter if they are false teachings. I'm afraid it would take nothing short of a miracle to get them to see the light."

"We could try to show them."

He smiled at her innocence. "You're precious, you know that?" He rubbed her chin. "Do you honestly think they would listen to me, who left to serve in the military? Or you, a young woman, who in their eyes, can be easily tempted?"

She shrugged.

"Tell me something, Rosanna. Would *you* be willing to leave the Amish if it meant following the Truth?"

"That is a hard question." She moved her hand over her belly. "It would be like throwing away our heritage, our…our relationships with all our family and friends. I don't know if I'd be strong enough to do that." She shook her head. "Do you have any idea how much heartache you caused when you left?"

"I can imagine. Really, I can. But don't you see? All that weeping and heartache could be avoided if they embraced the Truth. Mothers and fathers wouldn't be crying, thinking their children were doomed to Hell just because they'd chosen a different way of living. When you believe the Truth, there's an incredible freedom.

You're free to live without fear. You're free to choose to attend a church based on your God-given convictions. And if our Amish church embraced the Truth, there's no doubt in my mind that I would choose to attend the meetings. Amish culture has many positive aspects, but I cannot sacrifice the Truth of God's Word for the sake of heritage and tradition."

"Have you tried talking to your folks?"

"I've written letters to them. It's kind of like talking to a wall of stone. They will not hear what I have to say. They think I am living in sin."

"Are you?" She glanced at the television.

"You see this?" He walked over and touched the TV. "This will only show what I allow it to. It doesn't come on by itself. It only plays the stations I program it to play. Wanna see?"

She shook her head but he turned it on anyway.

"That man on there is talking about the Bible. He has studied the Bible for years." Zach explained.

"But that's not the only thing you watch?"

"I've rented good, Christian films that help build my faith. And yes, I could definitely use it to sin if I wanted to. But you don't need a TV to sin. Sin begins in the heart. If your heart is right, you won't *want* to sin. You'll want to please God."

"Is that what you want to do?"

"Yes, very much so. I want to live for God with all my heart."

"That is what I want to do too."

"Do you mean that?"

"*Jah*."

"Do you think it would please God if you asked Him to save you?"

"I do, but I already have trusted in Him. When I was reading earlier, I told God that I wanted to be saved."

Thank You, Lord Jesus. Thank You. "Really? That's wonderful!" He couldn't contain a brief embrace.

"I hope I said the right words."

"If they came from the heart, they were the right words."

"They did."

He shifted from one foot to another, then looked her in the eyes. "And do you think it would please God if you said yes to marrying me?"

She giggled. "You're the one proposing now?"

"It's the man's place, ain't so?"

She nodded. "In that case, I do. I think God would be pleased with that. And I think John would too."

"You realize what you're agreeing to?"

"If the Bible really is the Truth, I have nothing to lose."

"Do you want to marry me *now*?"

"Goodness." She placed a hand over her abdomen. "I think the baby just said yes."

"And what do *you* say?" He wanted to be absolutely certain of her feelings. Asking her to leave the church and marry him was a monumental step.

"My folks are going to be upset with me, but I want to. It think it is what God wants of me. He has given me peace." She stepped close enough to kiss him, but he refrained. "I want to become Mrs. Zachariah Zook."

"You don't know how happy it makes me to hear you

say those words. I never thought I'd hear them from you. But it seems both you and God have given me a second chance." He stared into her eyes and longed to kiss her, but he would wait until they were married. Despite his subsequent teasing, it was a promise he'd made to himself the day he first kissed her, thereby earning her scorn. He'd promised himself that if he ever got the chance again, he'd only kiss her on their wedding day. "Let's go talk to the pastor!"

Epilogue

"Oh, no, I think my water may have just broken!" Rosanna carefully lifted her expectant self from the sofa.

Zach's eyes widened as he appraised his wife's condition. She wasn't panicking, so he shouldn't either. "What does that mean? How much time do we have?"

"Judging from how my labor was with Johnny, we might have an hour." She grimaced. "I'll go get the hospital bag."

"An hour? Okay, let me call Betty. We can drop Johnny off on the way to the hospital. I'm sure he'd be happy to spend some time with Grandma." He pulled out his cell phone.

Two hours later, he was holding their sweet little girl in his arms. He imagined little Magdalena looked just like her momma when she was a newborn. What a joy to be able to hold his own flesh and blood.

"I think she has your eyes," Rosanna beamed with pride.

"You think so? I think she looks just like her beautiful momma." He bent down to meet his wife's lips, making sure not to smother the precious bundle of joy in his arms.

Commotion from behind him broke their special moment and he turned to see what was going on. *What on earth?*

He curiously eyed the two Amish couples. "*Mamm, Dat*? Isaac, Mary?" He looked to Rosanna to be sure he wasn't the only one having the vision.

His mother stepped forward. "Betty Brooks stopped by. She let us know where you were going and why. We asked Isaac and Mary if they'd like to join us." She looked at his father, then at Zach and Rosanna and smiled sheepishly. "I think the leaders will forgive us for this one transgression, *ain't so*?"

It had been over a year since they'd last seen their folks, but now here they were. It was a miracle, no doubt. They'd been blessed to have Frank and Betty Brooks as surrogate parents. Living close to them provided the support and love they'd been missing from their Amish families. And since Tommy had been their only son, Zachariah and Rosanna filled a void in their hearts as well.

Rosanna and Zach both still missed John like crazy. Last week had marked two years since his death. They'd gone to his gravesite and left flowers in his memory. Zach was certain that John would be pleased with the turn of events.

Zach smiled as little Johnny sat on the couch carefully holding his newborn sister in his arms. Being a father was a wonderful feeling. He couldn't help but wonder if John was looking down from Heaven and smiling too. Only one thing could describe the outcome of their lives—it had all been a result of God's sovereign grace.

* * * * *

A Special Thank You

I'd like to take this time to thank everyone that had any involvement in this book and its production, including Mom and Dad, who have always been supportive of my writing, my longsuffering Family-especially my handsome, encouraging Hubby, my former-Amish friends who have helped immensely in my understanding of the Amish ways, my supportive Pastor and Church family, my Proofreaders, my Editor, my CIA Facebook friends who have been a tremendous help, my wonderful Readers who buy, read, and leave encouraging reviews and emails, my awesome Street Team who, I'm confident, will 'Sprede the Word' about my books! And last, but certainly not least, I'd like to thank my Precious LORD and SAVIOUR JESUS CHRIST, for without Him, none of this would have been possible!

Chapter One

Elkhart County, Indiana

Deborah Miller ran to the clump of bare sycamore trees at the far edge of the pond on her family's property. Fortunately, the latest round of snow had melted, so she wouldn't be leaving tracks.

Several ducks squawked their disapproval of her presence. With indignation, they waddled and flapped onto the frozen water.

Deborah cringed. "Sorry to disturb you. I'll bring you some bread crusts tomorrow."

The largest tree in the grove had a tangle of many trunks from its base, creating an empty space in the center. She scurried over and dropped her green, tan, and white camouflage backpack into the hollow. A sprinkle of dried leaves on top, and no one would ever find it. Truth be told, she could leave her pack out in the open and no one would likely notice it. It would blend in with the tree's patchwork bark.

She took off running for the house between the stubbly, winter cornfield rows. She was going to be late. She'd lost track of time, which was her usual excuse, but this time was true. She could be gone all day and no one in her family ever noticed her absence. Or if they did, they never mentioned it. Apparently, keeping track of so many girls was too much trouble to bother with. Seven. And she was right smack dab in the middle. Not the oldest. Not the youngest. Not anything.

Of late, everyone was fussing over Hannah and Lydia, who were both planning to marry this fall. Although no one was supposed to know, for neither would be officially announced until late summer or early fall, but a lot of celery would be planted in the garden this spring. After all, they couldn't have Amish weddings without celery.

It had been a *gut* photo shoot today. The sun was shining, and though cold out, it had been a perfect day. Even if by some strange chance her absence had been noticed and she got scolded for being gone, it wouldn't dampen her mood. Nothing could spoil today.

Deborah pulled her coat tighter around herself as she slowed down and entered the yard, finding it oddly quiet. She needed to look as though she hadn't been in a hurry and just lost track of time, as usual.

Chickens pecked about the ground, but no people could be seen. Where was everyone? Were *all* her sisters in the house with *Mutter*? That was peculiar. One or two were often outside this time of day. Unusual to have caught them all in the kitchen.

An Amish man came out of the barn, carrying two empty buckets.

Who was he? She'd never seen him before. Though dressed Amish, she had to wonder if he belonged to their community. His light brown hair peeked out from under his black felt hat. The brim shaded his face. Just the type of rugged Amish man Hudson, her photographer, had repeatedly asked her to find for photo shoots. What was this stranger doing on their farm?

She approached him. "Who are you?" Her words puffed out on little white clouds.

"I'm Amos Burkholder. Who are you?" He smiled.

A warm, inviting, disarming smile. The kind that could make her forget her purpose. A smile she wouldn't mind retreating into. She mentally shook herself free of his spell. "I'm Deborah Miller. I live here. What are you doing on our farm? And where's my family?"

"Deborah? I was told the whole family went to the hospital. What are *you* doing here?"

"Hospital? Why?" Her family went to the hospital and hadn't noticed her absence? It figured.

"Bartholomew Miller had an accident. An ambulance came. Bishop Bontrager asked me to take care of things here until you all returned and your *vater* was able to work it again."

"My *vater*? Accident? What happened? Is he all right?"

"I don't know the details. But if the bishop thinks your *vater* will be well enough to work his farm again, then I think he will be all right eventually. Would you like me to drive you into Goshen to the hospital?"

Deborah shook her head. "If I hitch up the smaller buggy, I can drive myself."

"I'll hitch it."

"Danki." Deborah ran into the house to grab her bag of sewing. In case she had a while to wait at the hospital, she wanted to have something to keep herself distracted from too much worry. When she came back out, Amos wasn't much farther along in getting the buggy ready.

Impatient, Deborah stalked over to the horse standing in the yard and took hold of the harness on the other side from Amos.

He stopped his progress. "I'm capable of doing this myself."

Deborah hooked the belly strap. "I know." What Amish person didn't know how to hitch up a horse to a buggy by themself by age ten or twelve? "If I help, it'll go faster."

After a deep breath, he got back to the work at hand. Once the buggy was hitched and ready to go, he climbed in the side opposite her and took charge of the reins.

She put her hands on her hips. "What are you doing?"

"Taking you into town."

"I told you that I can drive a buggy myself."

"I know and have no doubt you're capable, but you're flustered over the news of your *vater*, and it would be best if you don't drive in your present state."

"Present state? What's that supposed to mean?"

He tilted his head. "Are you getting in? Or would you rather walk to town?"

With a huff, she climbed aboard and plopped down on the seat. "You are insufferable."

He handed her a quilt for her lap, then gently snapped the reins and clucked the horse into motion. "If by insufferable, you mean helpful, then *danki*."

Why was she being so ill-tempered? This wasn't like her. Maybe it was the news of her *vater* being injured. Or maybe it was her guilt of being away from the house when it happened. Or maybe it was because she knew she had been doing something her *vater*, family, and the community would frown upon. Or maybe it was all three. Whatever the reason, Amos didn't deserve her poor attitude when he was being so helpful and kind. "I'm sorry for being difficult. I'm worried about my *vater*."

"That's understandable."

She blew into her hands to warm them, then slipped on her knitted mittens. "I haven't seen you before. Do you belong to a neighboring community district?"

"*Ne*. We live on the other side of the district. We moved here a year ago from Pennsylvania. We're at church every other Sunday. You've even been to church at our farm. We obviously haven't made a memorable impression on you. Or at least I haven't."

How could she not remember him? "Tell me a little about your family to remind me."

"I am the youngest of five boys. The two oldest stayed in Pennsylvania and split the farm we had there."

"I think I know who you are or at least your family. I'm the middle of seven girls."

"I know. I've seen you in church along with all your sisters."

He'd noticed her?

"Tell me something. Is Miriam spoken for or being courted by anyone?"

So, he had his eye on her sister, who was a little over a year older than herself. So, it hadn't been Deborah he'd noticed at church but her sister. Disappointing. Someone else who overlooked her. "Timothy Zook seems interested in her."

"Is she interested in him?"

"Some days *ja* and others *ne*. Miriam likes a lot of boys. She can't seem to decide which one she likes most. She's so afraid of choosing the wrong man to marry, we fear she'll never marry at all." Deborah pulled a face. "I probably shouldn't have told you all that. Please don't hold it against her. She's a very wonderful sister."

His chuckle held no humor.

Was it truly Miriam she didn't want him to think poorly of or herself because of her derogatory words? Why should she care how this man thought of her? But she did. "Can you hurry? I need to know how my *vater* is."

"I'm going as fast as the *Ordnung* allows."

"But this is kind of an emergency. You would be allowed to go faster."

He thinned his lips. "This isn't an emergency. Your *vater's* being well looked after. Whether it takes us five minutes or five hours to get there will have no bearing on your *vater's* condition."

He was right, of course, but she had already missed so much. She very much wished she were going by car. "When was my *vater* hurt?"

"First thing this morning."

So long ago? He must have gotten hurt soon after she had slipped away. Now, she really did feel guilty.

Like Amos said, if she got to the hospital with everyone else or in the next hour, she wouldn't have been able to make a difference. But at least she could have been with her family. And know what was going on.

She settled her nerves for the plodding, boring journey. "Do you miss Pennsylvania?"

"Ne."

That was a sharp reply.

"But you grew up there. Your friends are there. The rest of your family is there. Don't you miss any of them?"

"Ne."

Again, his single word sounded harsh.

"There's nothing for me back there. This move was supposed to be *gut*."

But she sensed it wasn't. She wanted to press him to understand why he seemed to harbor bitterness toward the place where he'd grown up, but doubted he would tell her anything. After all, they were basically strangers.

Amos pulled in next to several other buggies outside the hospital.

She jumped out. "You don't have to stay. I'll get a ride back with my family. *Danki*." She trotted inside. She inquired at the information desk and soon found her family with all her sisters as well as several other community members. Her *vater* sat in a wheelchair, waiting to be discharged.

His left arm rested in a sling, and his left leg in a cast was propped on a pillow on one of the wheelchair's leg supports. He'd chosen neon green. Would the church leaders approve of the color? Probably not, but they wouldn't be able to do anything about it until he had the cast changed in a few weeks.

Thirteen-year-old Naomi made a face at her.

Deborah ignored her younger sister, who liked to stir up trouble, and hurried over to him. "*Vater*, are you all right?"

Vater gave her a lopsided smile. "I'm feeling great. They gave me something for the pain. But I don't have any pain."

"There you are, Deborah" Her *mutter* frowned. "I was wondering where you'd gotten off to. Did you go to the vending machines without telling me?"

Vending machines? Hadn't her *mutter* noticed that Deborah had only just now arrived? That she'd been absent all day? Was she truly invisible to her family? Did any of them even care? No wonder she could be gone for hours and hours without repercussions. No one ever realized her absence.

Amos joined them then. "How are you doing, Mr. Miller?"

Vater waved his hands aimlessly through the air. "It's Bartholomew. I don't have any pain."

Deborah turned to Amos. "I thought you left."

"If you would have waited, I would have walked in with you." He turned to *Mutter*. "I brought Deborah."

Mutter gave Deborah a double take. "You weren't here? Then where were you?"

Oh, dear. "I went for a walk, and before I knew it, I had gone farther than I realized, and it took me a while to get back home."

"Oh." *Mutter* turned back to the nurse behind *Vater's* wheelchair. "Are we leaving now? I want to leave now. I have supper to start."

"We need to wait for the doctor to sign the release papers."

How had any of them survived infancy and childhood with *Mutter* always forgetting things? Well, mostly forgetting Deborah. She didn't have trouble with the rest of her daughters. Just her middlest one.

The familiar pang of being left out twisted around her heart. One of these days, she might decide not to return. Would her *mutter* even notice? Probably not.

Well, it *had been* a perfect day until she'd come home and found out her world had been turned upside down.

Amos's inviting brown gaze settled on her. She wished now the buggy ride had taken longer. His look of sympathy warmed her heart. Well, at least *he* acknowledged her presence.

Amos studied Miriam, who smiled at everyone in the hospital waiting room. Did she truly like a lot of young men? Or was she just really nice? He'd been fooled by girls before. More than once. His gaze shifted back to Deborah. She stood on the edge of the crowd, with them but not really a part of them. How could no one have noticed she hadn't been with the family when they left for the hospital? Or at least once they arrived. He admired how she seemed to take that in stride. The hospital lights didn't spark the red hints in her hair the way the sun had done.

Deborah turned to him, and he smiled at her without

thinking. Her green eyes seemed as though she could see his broken heart. There was something more to her than met the eye. Something he couldn't quite figure out. Like she had some sort of secret. Probably just his own guilty conscience. He didn't want to look away, but he did.

From down the hall, a man stared at him. It was his cousin Jacob. His shunned cousin Jacob, who'd left the Amish church and community. He glanced back at the crowd of his fellow Amish waiting for Bartholomew to be released.

He moved around the crowd to Bishop Bontrager. "I have something I need to take care of. Will you let the Millers know that I'll meet them back at their farm?"

The bishop nodded. "*Ja. Danki* for agreeing to lend them a hand. Bartholomew is going to be laid up for some time. Will your *vater* be able to spare you to stay on at the Millers'?"

"*Ja.* I'm sure he can." His *vater* had already declared the farm not big enough for Amos. He glanced in the direction where Jacob had been. "I won't be far behind everyone." As he hurried down the hall, he threw a glance back over his shoulder at Deborah and almost went back to her but didn't. When he turned the corner, his cousin stood, leaning against the wall. Jacob looked strange but *gut* in his English clothes, jeans and a hooded sweatshirt. They suited his cousin. "What are you doing here?"

"I saw you drive up with one of the Miller girls. Quite a collection of Amish you're with. None of them *your* family though. *And* the bishop."

"Bartholomew Miller broke his leg." Amos glanced back to make sure no one had followed him. "The bishop asked me to help out at their farm while they took him to the hospital."

Jacob nodded. "You seemed pretty content with all of them. Are you still interested in leaving?"

Amos's insides knotted. This would be a life-changing decision, but he didn't see the use of the Amish life anymore. His *vater* didn't have land enough for all his sons, and the Amish girls here seemed no different from the flighty ones back in Pennsylvania. Except Deborah. She seemed different. But that was what he'd thought about Esther. And Bethany. "*Ja*, of course I am."

"It might take a few weeks to get everything set up. I'll be in touch with more information."

"I'll wait to hear from you." Once away from the community and no longer having to keep this a secret, he'd feel better about his decision. "I should go before they get suspicious." Amos could be shunned just for talking to an ex-Amish member. But once he left, he would be shunned and turned over to the devil and excommunicated from the church as well.

"See you soon." Jacob walked off in the opposite direction of the waiting room.

Amos peeked around the corner. None of his Amish brethren remained, only a handful of *Englishers*. He straightened before heading down the hall and out to the buggy parking area.

The only one that remained was the one he'd driven into town. Deborah sat on the buggy seat, rubbing her mitten-clad hands briskly together. She turned his direction, and his heart sped up.

He stopped beside the vehicle. Though she wore a *kapp*, the sun once again ignited the hints of red in her hair around her face. "What are you still doing here? Why didn't you go with the others?"

The quilt lay across her lap. "All the other buggies were full."

That was a little sad. She'd been left behind. Now, he felt bad for making her wait.

She picked up the reins and tilted her head. "Are you getting in? Or would you rather walk?"

Throwing his words back at him? Little scamp, but she'd lightened his mood. He climbed in and extended his hands for the reins.

She moved them from his reach and snapped the horse into motion.

He couldn't believe she just did that. She was audacious. "I should drive."

"Why?"

"Because I'm the man and you're a woman."

She set her jaw and kept control of the reins. "I'm quite capable, thank you."

She certainly seemed so, as well as a little bit feisty. He wanted to drive, but unless he wrestled the reins away from her, it didn't seem likely. "Did I do something to upset you?"

"Ne." Her answer was short and clipped.

"It certainly seems like I did. No one else around for you to be angry at."

She tossed the reins into his lap. "Take them if you want to drive so badly."

Now, he had vexed her. He didn't want the reins this way and was tempted to leave them where they lay, but that wouldn't do for the horse to have no guidance. With the reins in hand, he pulled to the side of the street in front of an antique store and stopped. "If I haven't upset you, then what has?"

She took a slow breath, and for a moment, he doubted she would answer him, but then she let out a huff of white air. "It doesn't matter."

"*Ja*, it does. Tell me." Why did it bother him so much that she was upset? He should just let it go and get back to her family's farm.

"My family went off to the hospital and didn't notice I wasn't with them."

That could be quite upsetting, but he'd thought that hadn't bothered her. He'd been wrong. "They were probably all worried about your *vater*. Focused on getting him the care he needed."

She sat quiet for a moment, and he could almost feel her mood shift. "You're right. I was being selfish. Only thinking of myself. I have a habit of doing that. *Danki*."

He smiled. *"Bitte."* He liked that he could help her and appreciated her honesty. Something he'd found lacking in others.

She waved her mittened hand in the air. "Shall we go?"

He lifted the reins but then paused and handed them over to her. "You can drive."

The smile she gifted him with and the spark in her green eyes as she took the reins warmed him all over.

Chapter Two

Amos sat forward on the buggy seat as the Miller farm came into view. What would people think of him not driving? He was the man after all. He *should* be driving. His instinct told him to take the reins, but something held him back. He gritted his teeth, hoping no one would be out in the yard.

Deborah pulled on one rein and slackened the other to turn into the driveway.

Though several buggies, the chickens, and two cats were scattered about the yard, fortunately, no people were in sight.

She stopped the buggy in front of the house. "Do you mind putting this away by yourself? I want to see how my *vater's* doing."

He gladly took the offered reins. "I'd be happy to." He breathed easier having the strips of leather in his hands. How foolish of him, but he couldn't help feeling that way. "Tell your *vater* not to worry about the animals. I'll take care of everything."

"*Danki*. But I think he probably still has enough pain medication in him to not worry about much of anything right now." She jogged up the porch steps and into the house.

He stared at the door a moment, feeling a sense of loss. But that couldn't be. He hadn't lost anything. At least not anything new. With a shake of his head, he drove the buggy to the barn. After unhitching the horse, he put the animal in a stall then parked the buggy in its space inside the barn. Being an open buggy, it needed to be protected from the elements. With the harness put away, he brushed down the horse and fed him.

His encounter with his cousin Jacob played in his head. He needed to get off his *vater's* farm and experience the outside world more than what he had on *Rumspringa*, with a different purpose this time. If he wasn't going to have land to farm and would have to work in the *Englisher* world anyway, he might as well live there too and be a part of it.

Amos would have left the first time when Jacob suggested it if there had been some place for him to go, but today was a different matter. The image of Deborah standing on the edge of her family at the hospital tugged at his heart. She needed him. This family needed him. Bartholomew needed him. And he needed them so he wouldn't have to be on his family's farm until he left for *gut*. This would make the wait more bearable.

He heard the humming of a female enter the barn. Deborah? He peeked out of the stall he was in as someone disappeared into the stall with the milking cow but couldn't tell who. He brushed down the front of his coat and trousers to remove hay particles, then stepped into the stall doorway.

Miriam glanced up at him with a smile from where she sat on a three-legged stool. "*Hallo*, Amos Burkholder."

His smile sagged a bit. "*Hallo*." This was *gut* that it wasn't Deborah. He shouldn't be thinking of her. "Your job to milk the cow?"

She leaned her head against the animal's side and began the task with a *swish-swish-swish*. "*Ja*."

"Do you and your sisters trade off with this duty?"

"*Ne*, I like milking. There is something soothing about it. It's just me and Sybil."

"I'm sorry. Would you like me to go away?"

"*Ne*."

He wasn't sure if he was disappointed or not at having to stay. "Tell me about your sisters."

"What do you want to know?"

"I don't know. I figure if I'm going to be working on your farm, I should know a little about everyone."

She nodded. "Hannah and Lydia are twins—identical. Hannah is the ultra-responsible one. Lydia is the peacemaker. They are both being courted and will likely get married this fall. Then comes me. A lot of people say I'm the positive one. I do try to see the *gut* in situations."

That's not how Deborah had described her. What was it she had said? That Miriam liked a lot of boys. Likely, there wasn't one young man in particular who had caught her attention yet.

"Then Deborah. After her comes Joanna. She's the *gut* one. Not that the rest of us aren't *gut*, but she was an easy baby and has always been easy to please. She's also quite shy. Naomi's thirteen and can be moody. She likes to be the center of attention. And lastly is carefree baby Sarah at eight. She is easily everyone's favorite, and the sweetest of us all."

Everyone got a description except Deborah. "What about Deborah?"

"What about her?"

"You gave everyone a little description except her."

"Did I? Hm. Deborah is…irres— rarely here."

Was she about to say irresponsible? True, Deborah hadn't been around when her *vater* had been hurt, but that didn't necessarily make her irresponsible.

When Miriam finished milking, Amos hoisted the full bucket and carried it to the house.

Miriam opened the door to the kitchen and allowed him to enter first. The kitchen bustled with female activity. He was used to just his *mutter* in the kitchen, alone, doing all the work by herself.

Deborah looked up from her task of churning butter with the youngest girl and smiled at him.

He responded in kind.

Her gaze flickered beside him where Miriam appeared, and Deborah's smile faltered, then she pushed her mouth up in a less genuine smile but one of encouragement.

He wished he could bring back that first smile. What had caused the change? More importantly, how could he bring back the first smile?

"Right this way, Amos." Miriam motioned with her

hand for him to follow her. "That goes in the back fridge until morning."

Amos aimed his apologetic shrug toward Deborah as he obediently complied. When he returned, Deborah's *mutter* stood in his path.

Teresa Miller put her hands on her hips and gave him an impish smile. "We do so love company, but you can't walk through my kitchen without introducing yourself."

"I'm Amos Burkholder."

"Which one of my daughters are you courting?"

"Um…none. I'm here to help out on the farm while Bartholomew is healing."

Shock and concern wiped away the older woman's smile in an instant. "What? What's wron—?"

One of the older girls hooked her arm around her *mutter's* shoulders and escorted her out of the kitchen. "Let's go see how *Vater* is doing."

Another of the older sisters stood in front of him. "Supper will be ready in a little bit. We'll call you when it's ready."

This must be Lydia, the peacemaker. The one who left with their *mutter* must have been Hannah, the ultra-responsible one. Or it could be vice versa. He wasn't sure. He nodded and went back outside to finish up some chores.

Soon, another one of the sisters came out to retrieve him. "Supper's ready." She kept her head down.

"*Danki.* I'll head in with you." He walked to her side. "I didn't mean to upset your *mutter* earlier."

Her head remained down and her voice soft. "You didn't. She was just worried about *Vater.*"

It had seemed more than worry. But then what did he know?

This shy girl must be Joanna. It would probably be best if he didn't stress her by trying to hold a meaningless conversation just to fill the silence.

Inside, he washed up and waited to be told where he should sit at the table.

Bartholomew sat alone at the far end of the table. His broken leg propped up on a chair. The women still scurried to and fro.

The youngest, who looked to be more like five than eight, crashed into him and wrapped her chubby arms around his waist. "Broffer Amos."

He wasn't sure what to make of this little one. "*Hallo*, Sarah."

She giggled.

One of the twins, he guessed Lydia, hurried over and disentangled the young one from him. "I'm sorry about that. She likes to greet people with a hug."

"That's all right." He gazed down into the upturned face of Sarah. Her slanted eyes and flat nose told him all he needed to know. Down syndrome. "I'm very pleased to meet you."

Lydia smiled at him but spoke to Sarah. "Go sit down. It's time to eat."

Sarah grabbed his hand. "Sit by me."

He looked to Lydia, who gave him a nod. He sat down and quickly the others did so as well. Bartholomew blessed the food, and everyone served themself except Sarah. Hannah, who sat on her other side, dished up for her.

Bartholomew grimaced in pain. His medication had probably worn off. "Amos, I certainly do appreciate you coming to help out in my hour of need."

"I'm glad to be here."

Teresa tilted her head. "Hour? It'll be a mite more than that." Her anxiety from earlier erased.

The girl directly across from Amos crinkled her nose. "I bet you don't even know who all of us are."

Center of attention. "You're Naomi."

He went around the table and named each of the family members.

Naomi narrowed her eyes. She obviously didn't think he could do it.

He wasn't so sure himself but had guessed right. Miriam's descriptions had helped. When he'd named Deborah and she smiled at him, something inside did a little flip. That was the smile he'd been looking for. He'd wanted to stop and stare at her but knew he shouldn't.

He cleared his throat to clear his head as well and shifted his attention to Bartholomew. "I could, of course, travel home each night and return in the morning, but I would be able to get more work accomplished if I stayed on here."

Bartholomew swallowed his mouthful of food. "What did you have in mind?"

"I thought I could sleep in the barn."

Teresa spoke up. "I won't hear of that. The barn is no place for a person in winter."

Bartholomew gazed gently at his *frau*. "What would you suggest, *Mutter*?"

"Joanna and Naomi can move in with Miriam and…"

She waved her hand in Deborah's direction. "And her sister."

A sadness flickered across Deborah's face, and Amos's heart ached for her. He knew what it was like to be hurt by family.

Naomi leaned forward. "I don't want to move rooms and be crowded in."

"Hush," Bartholomew scolded his daughter, who huffed and folded her arms. Then he turned back to his *frau*. "You would have a young man who isn't a family member under the same roof as our daughters?"

Teresa's gaze flittered around the table, and the inappropriateness of the situation registered on her face. "Oh. I…"

Amos didn't want to cause a fuss. "I don't want to displace anyone. The barn will be fine. There's an old woodstove still connected in the tack room. I can move a few things around and set up a cot." It was preferable to home.

With supper concluded and the arrangements settled, he headed out to fix up his new but temporary living quarters.

He located some firewood and lit the stove. Then he made a clearing in the center of the room and set up the cot that was used when an animal was sick and someone needed to stay in the barn to keep a watchful eye out.

A gray tabby rubbed against his leg. He crouched and petted him. "What's your name, hmm?"

The cat sauntered over to the stove, sniffed it, and laid down in front of it.

"Don't get too comfortable. You can't stay in here

at night with the door closed. You can warm yourself until I find some blankets."

When he exited the tack room, Deborah stood outside his door with an armful of quilts. She smiled. "We thought you might need these." She handed him the pile. "There's a pillow as well."

"*Danki*. These'll be better than the horse blankets I was planning to rustle up."

"*Bitte*." Her gaze lingered on him a long moment before she turned to leave.

He wanted to say something to make her stay. But what use would there be in that? Instead, he watched her walk out.

The following morning, Deborah stole glances at Amos throughout breakfast. Several times, she caught him looking back at her.

Vater hadn't come to the table for breakfast. Fortunately, his and *Mutter's* bedroom was on the main floor, so he wouldn't have to get up and down the stairs with a broken leg and injured arm. Though *Mutter* had scurried around the kitchen earlier, she had gone in to sit with *Vater*. Since *Vater's* accident, less than a day ago, *Mutter* acted stranger than usual. One moment she sat calmly, and the next she scampered about like a nervous squirrel looking for lost acorns.

Amos drained the last of his coffee. "*Danki* for breakfast. I should get to work."

"Would you like another cup?" For some reason, she didn't want him to leave yet. It was nice having another man around the farm. Or was it that it was just different for all the girls? Or was it having a kind, handsome, eligible man around?

His mouth curved up into a smile that tickled her insides. "*Danki*. Maybe later." He gazed at her a moment before trudging outside.

After he left, she stared at the door for a bit longer than she should before she turned. "What do you need me to do?"

Lydia had taken charge of the kitchen clean up. "I think we have everything covered."

Her sisters bustled around, busy at work. Even Naomi helped, and Sarah had her little job of sorting the silverware. The only other one not there besides their parents was Hannah.

Deborah headed for her parents' room and peeked in around the doorframe. "Is there anything I can do? Anything you need?"

Mutter held a plate while *Vater* ate with his *gut* arm.

Hannah gingerly tucked a pillow under *Vater's* broken leg. "We're *gut*. See if the others need help in the kitchen."

Deborah gave a weak smile. She'd already done that. "*Vater*, I'm praying you heal quickly."

"*Danki*."

She left. With nothing to do inside, she headed outside and found Amos in the barn.

He stood under the hayloft, staring up at the under side of the floor above.

"What are you doing?"

Turning to her, his mouth pulled up on the corners. "Trying to decide the best way to fix this."

She liked his smile. A lot. She stood next to him and looked to where he pointed. A hole roughly the size of a laundry basket had been broken through several of the boards, and hay hung down in the opening. "What happened?"

Shifting, he stared at her. "You really don't know?"

"Know what?"

"Your *vater* fell through there and landed here on the floor. Fortunately, there weren't any tools, boxes, or barrels for him to get further injured on."

She pictured her *vater* falling and gasped. She hadn't thought to ask just how he'd gotten hurt. All she knew was that he had fallen.

"The boards look pretty rotted. They should have been replaced long before now."

"Why hadn't he done that?"

"He was probably too busy with running the rest of the farm on his own to notice. I'll check all the boards and build a new loft floor if need be. I figure I can do some of the regular maintenance he couldn't get to and repair what needs repairing until I…until it's time to plow and plant."

"Do you think he's going to be in a cast that long?"

"Hard to say. Some people's bones heal faster than others. But even if he's out of the cast, his leg will be weak. He'll need time to regain his strength."

"What can I do to help?"

He chuffed out a chuckle. "What? I'm sure there's plenty to be done in the house."

"Hannah and Lydia are taking care of *Vater* while overseeing the breakfast clean up as well as the early prep for lunch. Everyone's busy with their regular duties, leaving nothing for me except free time." She didn't even have a modeling job today. That would have been nice to get her mind off *Vater* being hurt.

"This isn't woman's work."

"If you haven't noticed, my *vater* has seven girls. We've all done a bit of carpentry, livestock tending, and even some plowing. So, let me help."

"*Danki* for the offer, but I can manage."

If she were a man, he'd accept her help. "Well, I have nothing else to do, so I'm not leaving." She backed up to a covered feed barrel, pushed herself up and sat. "If you won't let me help with the labor, I'll supervise from here." The truth was, she just wanted to be out here with him.

He stared at her hard for a long moment. "*You* are going to tell *me* how to fix this?"

"It's either that or put me to work." The work would go faster if he allowed her to help. Would he be too stubborn and insist on doing it alone? If so, he deserved to have a more difficult time than need be, *and* he deserved to have her comment on every little thing he did.

"Fine. But you have to do as I say. I don't want you getting hurt as well."

She hopped off the barrel and saluted him.

He shook his head at her playful gesture. "First we need to determine how sturdy the rest of this floor is." He handed her a shovel, and he grabbed a pitchfork for himself. "Tap the underside of the boards with the end of the handle." He demonstrated with his implement.

Deborah poked at a board to show him that not only

did she understand his elementary instructions, but that she could follow his directions as ordered. Then she smiled.

His mouth worked back and forth, presumably to keep from smiling himself. His effort created a cute expression.

She studied her shovel from tip to end. She didn't like the idea of lifting the heavy metal blade up and down. The repetitive movement would give her sore muscles, for sure. After looking around, she leaned the shovel against the wall and grabbed the push broom handle. Putting her foot on the head, she twisted the handle several times, freeing it. This was lighter. Much better for repetitive motions. She twirled it around once and went to work tapping and poking. "Tell me about your family."

Amos shrugged. "Like what?"

"Parents. Siblings."

"I have two parents and four brothers."

Not very forthcoming with information. She was going to have to work harder at learning anything about him. She would start with something easy and hope he got the hint and freely offered up more details. "What are your parents' names?"

"Joseph and Karen."

At least half the boards she poked at were usable for the time being but would need to be replaced soon. The other half of them were splintery and soft. "What about your brothers?"

"James, Boaz, Daniel, and Titus."

She felt like growling and poking *him* with a stick.

Couldn't he give her more information? Did he not want to talk to her? Well, she wasn't about to work in silence. Her sisters chatted all the time while doing chores. "Where do you fit in to all of them?"

"Youngest."

Really? Nothing more than that? She did growl now, softly to herself and jabbed her stick at the next board. It poked through, splintering the wood in half. Hay showered down on her from between the dangling halves.

Amos rushed over and pulled her out of the way as one of the jagged pieces broke free and shot straight down to where she'd been standing. She could have been seriously injured.

Caught off guard by his action, she lost her balance and grabbed at his sleeve. Her body twisted, and gravity did the rest of the work, landing her in a pile of straw.

Between her yanking on his sleeve and his trying to catch her, he lost his footing as well and landed in the straw beside her with one arm stretched across to the other side of her. His eyes stretched wide. "Are you all right? Did you get hurt?"

He looked so adorable all worried like, that a giggle escaped her lips before she could stop it.

His mouth pulled up on the corners. "I guess that means you're not hurt."

She nodded and wrestled her chortling under control.

He plucked hay off her cheek and forehead. "You're covered."

She imagined she was but didn't help him, liking his ministrations.

His hand stilled, and he stared down at her for a long moment.

What was he thinking?

Clearing his throat, he pushed himself up to his feet, then offered her assistance. His hand was large and strong. And warm.

As soon as she was on her feet, he released her quickly as though embarrassed and stared up at the ceiling. "Too many of the boards are rotted beyond repair, and the ones that are serviceable won't be for long. It would be best to replace the whole floor. I'll take the wagon into town and order the necessary lumber."

Now he was chatty? Or had their little moment made him uncomfortable? She missed the moment of closeness they'd just shared. Would they have another one in the future? She hoped so.

Chapter Three

The next morning, Amos had been sent into town by the oldest twin, Hannah, to pick up some medicine for Bartholomew Miller. Though identical in most respects, he noted that Hannah had a worry crease between her eyebrows, which helped him to differentiate the two sisters.

He now drove back along the paved road. Floyd plodded along. The rhythm of his clip-clopping hoof beats lulled Amos's thoughts. Thoughts that drifted to his cousin. Jacob was *gut* to help Amos. Amos wouldn't know what to do on the outside. Having his cousin's guidance made him feel easier about the whole endeavor. Jacob knew all about Amos's hurts back in Pennsylvania. How Esther had let him court her and led him believe she cared for him, only to turn down his offer of marriage. Then when he'd arrived in Indiana, his past nearly repeated itself with Bethany.

Then his thoughts turned to the Millers' farm. The work there was *gut*. Gave him purpose. And being around all those women would give him insight into the female mind. Maybe then, he could figure out what he'd done wrong in the past.

Up ahead, an Amish woman meandered in the middle of the two-lane country road.

What was she doing?

A car came down the road, honked, and swerved around her.

She sidestepped but didn't move to the side of the road.

He snapped the reins to hurry the horse. When he pulled up beside her, he said, "Ma'am?"

She faced him but didn't really look at him.

"Teresa? Teresa Miller?" He hauled back on the reins.

"Ja." She raised her hand to shade her eyes from the morning winter sun.

"What are you doing out here?"

"I was going somewhere." She chuckled. "But I seem to have forgotten where."

That didn't explain why she was in the middle of the road. He jumped down. "Come. I'll drive you home."

"That would be nice. *Danki.*" She climbed into the buggy and waited.

How odd. But other than her being in the middle of the road, he couldn't put his finger on what exactly was off about this encounter. He got in and took her home.

When he drove into the yard and up to the house, the twins rushed outside without coats on. Hannah opened the buggy door and took Teresa's hand. *"Mutter,* where have you been? We've been looking for you." A forced cheeriness laced her words.

"I went for a nice little walk." She patted Amos's arm. "But I was safe."

Hannah helped her *mutter* out and exchanged glances with Lydia. Hannah's gaze flickered to him. *"Danki."*

"Bitte." Amos held out the paper sack with the prescription. "Here's your *vater's* medication."

Lydia took it. *"Danki."* The women rushed into the house, leaving Amos to wonder.

Women. They behaved strangely. How was a man to figure them out? Maybe it was impossible, and he should give up on them all together.

A while after Miriam had completed the late afternoon milking, Amos headed to the house for supper. Though he'd been mulling over this morning's incident with Teresa all day and wanted to ask about it, he decided not to embarrass her by mentioning anything.

He stepped through the kitchen door into barely ordered chaos. One girl went this way while another went that way and two others looked to be on a collision course but both swerved in the appropriate direction and barely missed running into each other. The women seemed to almost read each others' minds. Each one going in a different direction. How did they ever get anything accomplished? But somehow they managed to pull supper together .

Maybe there was some order to their mayhem he couldn't detect. That men in general couldn't. He would like to figure it out but sensed he could spend a lifetime and never understand women. He should give up even trying anymore.

Teresa Miller smiled and came over to him. "My brother stopped by and brought some of your things. They are in a suitcase by the front door."

"*Your* brother?"

"*Ja.* David. He wore that blue shirt I made him for his birthday."

Hannah gave a nervous sounding giggle, and the crease between her eyebrows deepened. "She meant *your* brother."

He didn't have a brother David. Maybe she meant his brother Daniel.

"*Ne.* I didn't—"

Lydia put her arm around Teresa, effectively distracting her. "*Mutter*, did you get the cake frosted?" The two walked to the far side of the kitchen.

Why did the twins seem nervous? Calling someone by the wrong name was common enough. Most everyone had done it. How many times had he been called by one of his brothers' names? If he had a cookie for every time, he'd be fat.

Hannah spoke to Amos. "Why don't you take your suitcase out to the barn? It's going to take a few minutes to get everything on the table."

Was she trying to distract *him*?

"All right." He snagged the case and headed out to the barn. That had been strange. But then this had been a bit of a strange day. And he was surrounded by women who didn't behave or think like men. They were mysterious creatures, whose sole purpose was to confuse and distract men.

He set the case on his bed and saw out of the corner of his eye the tabby dart in. When he turned to look, the cat dashed back out. What had scared it? He leaned to look on the other side of the potbelly stove where the cat had run from.

A tiny kitten with its eyes still closed lay on the ground. It raised its wobbly head and let out a small mew.

Amos picked it up. "Where has your *mutter* gone?" It seemed females of all species acted strange. He stepped out of the room and scanned the dim interior of the barn.

From the hayloft, the tabby trotted down the slanted ladder with another kitten hanging from her mouth. She ignored Amos and darted into his room. She quickly came back out and meowed at him. Then she put her paws on his leg and meowed again.

"I have your little one." He crouched down, and she took the kitten from him.

He followed her into the tack room. "How many little ones do you have?"

She obviously liked the warmth of the stove for her babies. She looked from him to beside the stove and back again.

He waved his hand. "Go on. Get the others. I'm not going to make you sleep in the cold."

She darted out.

Amos snagged an unused crate, put in a layer of straw, and then an old towel. By the time the *mutter* cat returned with number three, Amos had the crate with the two kittens in it next to the heat.

The tabby peered over the edge of the box, jumped in with the third kitten and laid down.

"I'll figure out how to keep the door open and stay warm later."

When he headed back to the house, all the girls sat silently at the table, hands folded in their laps. No one fluttered about. He could have waited until later to take out his suitcase. It didn't matter now. He sat next to Sarah as before.

As well as Bartholomew, Teresa and one of the twins weren't at the table. Which twin was here? She had the crease between her eyebrows, so she must be Hannah.

After the blessings, Hannah jumped right into conversation. "Now tell me about the barn. Are you comfortable out there? If you would rather return home, I'm sure we can manage. You must miss your family."

He actually didn't miss his family as much as he'd imagined he might, and he preferred the barn to home. Maybe leaving the community wouldn't be as hard as he anticipated. "I'm quite comfortable. *Danki*."

Hannah continued. "We wouldn't want to keep you or put your parents in a bad position by insisting you stay."

He glanced around the table. Except for Deborah and Miriam, the younger girls paid no attention to Hannah's words. "My parents and brothers can manage quite well without me." His brothers would be running the farm soon enough without me, might as well start now.

Deborah glanced from Hannah to Miriam, seemingly trying to figure things out as well. She shook her head and went back to eating.

Miriam stared hard at him and then stabbed a cooked carrot. "If you change your mind, we'll understand."

Distraction, and now, more than one sister appeared to be trying to get rid of him? Eligible women were always trying to get rid of him. Women were strange indeed. "I won't. I promised Bishop Bontrager that I would work here while your *vater* is recovering." If he weren't planning to leave all together, he might be tempted to ask Bartholomew if he wanted to hire him on afterward to help ease his burden.

Neither Hannah nor Miriam seemed pleased with his answer. Didn't they want their *vater* to have help?

Typical strange behavior for women.

The following Monday, Deborah studied Amos as he watched Miriam. Her sister stood at the clothesline hanging the laundry. She didn't know he was observing her. And *he* didn't know that Deborah was studying him.

How fortunate for Miriam to have someone look at her the way Amos did. Maybe someday someone would regard her in such a manner. But probably not. At least not in her Amish community. The only time she'd ever been noticed was in the *Englisher* world.

Tugging her coat closed, she slipped out past the garden that had been harvested and canned last summer and fall. Spring planting was still a couple of months off.

She hurried out to the cluster of bare sycamore trees

near the pond at the edge of their property. After retrieving her backpack from the tangled base of the largest tree, she headed for the meeting spot. No one would miss her. They never did. *Vater's* trip to the hospital had been proof of that.

Deborah tramped through the still fallow field. This year would be the year this field was planted again. She came out the other side and dashed down the road. At the intersection, an idling car waited. She opened the passenger door and climbed in. Then she switched to English. "Sorry for making you wait."

The older woman pointed toward Deborah's seatbelt. "I don't go any where until your seatbelt is on."

Deborah grabbed the belt, pulled it, and snapped it into place. One of the many differences between automobile travel and riding in a buggy.

The woman put her car into gear and pulled out onto the road. "I thought you might not be coming, and I was about to leave."

Deborah was glad the woman hadn't. "Thank you for waiting."

"This is certainly a strange place to be picked up. I've driven a lot of you Amish and always go to a house, not the side of the road."

"I didn't want to bother anyone." Deborah hoped the woman didn't suspect she was sneaking out. Deborah usually had another woman drive her, one who didn't ask so many questions or insinuate things.

She was relieved when the woman dropped her off at her destination. "Thank you for the ride." She paid the woman for her gas and time.

"Do you need me to come back and return you to where I picked you up?"

"No, thank you. I have a ride." Fortunately, her regular person could take her back.

She hustled away from the car before she could be further delayed and nearly ran into an *Englisher* woman with multicolored hair. "*Entschuldigen Sie*—I mean, excuse me."

The young woman stared a moment as though trying to figure out who Deborah was before she scurried away.

Deborah shrugged and ducked into the gas station convenience store restroom to change from her plain Amish dress into a pair of jeans and a sweatshirt and let down her hair. Where it had been twisted into place in the front it kinked and waved where it had been coiled in the back. When she wore these clothes with her hair freed, she felt like a different person. What would Amos think of her appearance? Disapprove, for sure.

She hurried to the photography studio and entered silently.

Hudson stood behind his camera giving instructions to the model sitting on a fake rock wall in front of a backdrop featuring an old building. He had dozens of such roll-down backdrops. From urban to countryside, woodlands to deserts to mountains, all four seasons and various weather, and fantasy backdrops with mythical creatures, medieval castles, gothic arches, a waterfall, and stone stairways in the forest.

Hudson, in his late twenties, had ambitions to move to New York City and become a famous photographer.

His wavy, shoulder-length, blond hair and dashing good looks said he could likely succeed on the other side of the camera as well. When she'd first started modeling for him a year ago, she'd developed a crush from all his praise and attention. Two things she rarely received at home.

His assistant, Summer, was the first to see her approaching. She leaned in and spoke to Hudson in a hushed voice.

He pulled back from his camera and swung Deborah's direction. "ebo! There you are."

When she hadn't wanted to use her real name, Hudson had dubbed her Débo. She didn't much care for it, but it was better than using Deborah and risk being discovered. No Amish would guess that was her even if they ever found out. The likelihood that any of them would see her in one of these *Englisher* catalogues was slim to none. If they did, they wouldn't recognize her.

He walked over to her and gripped her shoulders. "You're my best model. Go see Lindsey and Tina for wardrobe, hair, and make-up." He stared at her a little longer. Probably assessing the condition of her features today.

"What is it? Is something wrong?"

"It just amazes me how different you look from when you go into the dressing room and when you come out again. Lindsey and Tina are miracle workers. If I didn't know both women were you, I would never guess you were the same person."

Deborah counted on that. If her Amish brothers and sisters knew about this, she would be shunned. If the media found out she was an Amish girl modeling, they would exploit that. But Hudson and his team kept her secret, and as long as they did, she could continue to model. She wasn't hurting anyone and wasn't doing anything illegal. The money she earned would help her and her future husband buy a house and farm. She would quit as soon as someone special took interest and asked to court her.

Today's shoot was for a high-end clothing catalogue. She would be plied with make-up, and her hair would be curled and fluffed. It was fun to be pampered like this. It still gave her a chuckle at the variety of clothes the English owned and wore, different clothes for every season, every occasion, and various times of day.

For her, spring and summer meant she could put away her sweater and coat and didn't wear shoes or stockings most of the time, going barefoot. Same dress, just fewer layers. Her biggest decision was whether to wear her green, blue, or yellow dress. She wore far more outfits on a single photo shoot than she owned. Where did *Englishers* put them all? She would hate to have to wash the lot.

Once she had been rendered unrecognizable and dressed in a long flowing, summer dress she could never imagine owning, she returned to the main area of the studio.

Hudson smiled at her. "There's my favorite model." He positioned her in the shot and took lots of pictures. Same instructions he usually gave her.

Strange to be wearing a summer dress in the middle of winter. Strange to be wearing an *Englisch* summer dress period. She moved automatically and let her mind wander. Back to her family's farm. Was Amos still gazing at Miriam? Had her sister taken notice of his attention? Part of her hoped not.

Deborah focused on the hand snapping in front of her face.

Hudson stood less than a foot away. "You're distracted, Débo. I don't know where you were, but I need you here."

Was she distracted? *Ja.* She supposed she was. "I'm sorry." Her mind kept flittering back to Amos. Why? He wasn't her beau. Until a little over a week ago, she'd barely known he existed. Now, she couldn't shake him from her thoughts. He was like a mouse in the wall, always scratching. Always capturing her attention. Always crawling into her daydreams.

She tried to push Amos from her thoughts and focused on Hudson's instructions.

After four hours of changing clothes and hairstyles and having hundreds of photos taken of her, relief washed over Deborah to have the shoot over. After changing into her own English clothes and scrubbing her make-up off, she left the dressing room.

Hudson gathered the five models around him. "A mostly great shoot today." He gave Deborah a pointed look.

Her performance was in the part not included in the "mostly great."

"I need all of you back here tomorrow and for the rest of the week. The client wants the photos this weekend to present to his marketing department Monday."

The other models grabbed their coats and purses and headed out.

Deborah hung back. "I don't know if I can come every day."

He gave her a hard look. "Débo, I need you. You have to come."

"I'll try."

Surprisingly, she did manage to escape the farm each day, although some days were more of a challenge than others.

On Friday, Hudson praised them all for their hard work.

Deborah headed for the exit with aching feet and body. Her body from constantly moving, and her feet from being shoved into impractical shoes. Her brain hurt as well from repeatedly forcing Amos out of her thoughts.

"Débo, hold up." Hudson trotted over to her. "You want to grab a cup of coffee?"

How many times in the past had she hoped for just such an invitation? She shook her head. "I'm sorry, Hudson. I need to get home."

"But we ended early. Certainly you don't have to rush off so soon?"

"I have been gone too much from home this week." Not that her family noticed her absence. "And you have photos to edit for your client."

"Next Wednesday, then? I have a shoot. I'll see you then."

She shook her head again. "I need to stick around home for a while."

"If you had a phone, I could call you with opportunities."

She couldn't risk him calling their phone. That would

be disastrous for her. She finally escaped, all the while her mind wandering back to Amos.

Amos looked out over the Millers' fields to be plowed in the spring. He couldn't help but think of them as partly his. Since he'd already planned out the plowing and planting, they sort of felt a little like his fields. Of course, they weren't *his* field, and he might not even be here to do the work. But if he was, he would take pride in that work.

Bartholomew appreciated everything he did around the farm, so Amos worked harder and enjoyed it so much more here than he ever had at home.

Here, even the little things he did mattered. *He* mattered. Bartholomew had never had a son to help him with all the work around the farm. How had he run this place without sons?

But on the flip side, Amos's *mutter* was alone doing the house chores, cooking, cleaning, laundry for six men and boys through the years. How did *she* do it without help?

On the far side of one of the fields, a woman emerged from a bare stand of sycamore trees nestled next to a pond. She walked across the field he would plow in the not to distant future. If he was still here. Bartholomew should have his cast off by then, but he wouldn't likely be up for all the physical work yet. Maybe Amos should stay long enough to help with that.

The woman came closer and closer.

Deborah.

Where did she go all the time? She had disappeared every day this week and would be gone for hours. He was about to find out.

With her head down, she didn't see him approaching. He stepped directly into her path a few yards in front of her. She seemed to be talking to herself, but he couldn't make out all the words. Something about nothing wrong and not hurting anyone.

She kept walking with her head down. The words became clearer. "Everything will be fine. No harm done."

When it looked as though she might literally run into him, he cleared his throat.

She halted a foot away and jerked her head up. So startled to see him there, she took a step back and appeared to lose her balance on the uneven ground. Her arms swung out to keep herself up right.

He reached out and took hold of her upper arms to stop her from tumbling to the ground. "Whoa there."

She gasped. "I'm sorry. I didn't see you."

"Where have you been all day?"

"What? Nowhere." She tried to pull free of his grip, but he held fast.

He shook his head. "You've been somewhere. You've left every day this week and been gone for most of the day."

"I-I went for a walk."

"Where? Ohio?"

She twisted her face a moment before his joke made sense. "We have a pond just over there by those trees. I like to sit there and watch the ducks. It's a nice place to think and be alone. You should go some time."

"I did. Today. You weren't there."

Her self-satisfied expression fell. "I was for a while, then I walked farther."

He sensed there was more to her absence than a walk. "Where?"

"Why do you care?"

"With your *vater* laid up, I'm kind of responsible for everyone on this farm."

She rolled her eyes. "I'm fine. I can take care of myself."

How could she not understand the role of a man?

"May I go now?"

He realized he still held onto her upper arms. He didn't want to let her go but did. "I don't want you to leave the farm without telling me where you're going."

"Are you serious?"

He gave her his serious look.

She huffed and strode away.

Would she heed his request?

Where *did* she go every day? He had wanted to follow her, was tempted to, almost did once, but he had realized it was none of his business and turned around. But curiosity pushed hard on him. He still might follow her if she didn't obey. Just to see. Just to watch her from a distance. Just to know her secret.

Something inside him feared for her. Feared she would walk out across this field and never return. Feared her secret would consume them both. She was a mystery.

A mystery he was drawn to solve.

Deborah heaved a sigh of relief. She marched the rest of the way through the field, resisting the urge to run. Two weeks, and Amos Burkholder already paid more attention to her comings and goings than her own family did her whole life, who never expected much from her and thought her an airhead. Fanciful. Her head full of dreams and nonsense.

Well, she did have dreams. And to prove to everyone that she was someone to be noticed, not an airhead, she'd become a church member younger than any of her older sisters at age sixteen, the same year as Miriam who was a year and a half older than her. She'd basically skipped her *rumspringa*. But Naomi had run away in a fit of selfishness and sent the family into a tizzy. Miriam hadn't seem to mind having her special day of joining church ruined, but Deborah had.

No one had congratulated her or told her how wonderful it was that she'd joined so young, that she must be the most dedicated Amish woman ever. Anything to be noticed, just once.

Instead, the whole community had gone on a search for Naomi and found her, hours later, sulking under their porch. She'd walked home by herself, having somehow slipped out of the service, probably under the guise of needing to use the bathroom. She'd stayed hidden even when she'd known people were searching for her. She hated that so much attention was being paid to others.

It had been the last straw for Deborah. She'd tried to get her parents' attention and had given up several times, but she'd thought joining church so young would get their attention for sure. If only for a moment. She had just about succeeded until Naomi had pulled her disappearing act. Even after their parents had scolded her younger sister, Deborah gave her a round of her own. After that, Naomi made sure to steal any attention that might be portioned out to Deborah.

Deborah decided that with Naomi always wanting the most attention, Deborah would never get her fair share, so she'd decided to take advantage of being the invisible one. She let Naomi suck up all the attention she could get from the family. Sarah, being the baby and having Down syndrome, naturally got a goodly portion of attention as well. Joanna and Miriam both took everything in stride and seemed to almost be invisible as well, but they seemed to love it, as though it were their crowning glory to be overlooked. Always quietly in the background.

Well, that wasn't *gut* enough for Deborah. Wasn't she as important as any of the others? Wasn't she just as much in need of being noticed? Wasn't she as worthy as any of the others?

So, she took advantage of her invisibility and realized that her family never really noticed when she wasn't there. If it had been her missing that day instead of Naomi, when would her family have noticed? Certainly not as soon as they had for Naomi. It might not have been until the family was ready to leave for home in the late afternoon, instead of before the service even ended. Maybe not even until nightfall when she wasn't in her bed. Maybe never. But Hudson noticed her.

She had experimented with being gone from the family for longer and longer periods of time, until she could be gone all day without hardly a notice. She would claim to go for a walk and be gone for hours. When she returned home, she would be told to get her head out of the clouds and keep track of time. Didn't she know they worried about her? Worried? But they never came looking for her. When she told them that, they said she'd always been a wanderer and she always came home and she could take care of herself.

She had to admit that she had been self-sufficient from an early age. Everyone attributed it to when her *mutter* was so sick while carrying Joanna, that even at two, she somehow knew something had been wrong with *Mutter*, and it was best if she didn't cause a fuss. She'd learned to be quiet from all the shushing from adults and her three older sisters at ages four and three. They all knew to be quiet and not cause any more trouble for the family.

So, Deborah wandered farther and farther from home. Until she ended up at the edge of a photo shoot over a year a go.

Though she tried to stay hidden, the photographer, Hudson, had seen her and said she'd be perfect for the shot. A contrast between two worlds, the outside— *Englisher* world—and the Amish one. She hadn't wanted to do it. She knew she shouldn't. Hudson told her that there would be no harm in it. That none of her Amish people would ever know.

She'd thrilled at the idea of being special, being different. At being noticed. At no longer being invisible.

Hudson praised her and told her that she was a natural and followed direction better than most of his models. He'd paid her money for taking the pictures. He'd asked her to come to another shoot the following week. She said she couldn't, but then she found she couldn't resist and went. Soon, she participated in weekly shoots with him. After nearly two months, he asked her to change into *Englisher* clothes. She couldn't do that, could she? But she did. And she had enjoyed it.

Like being a different person with each new outfit. She wasn't hurting anyone and earned money for her future.

The clothes were always modest, but sometimes they put make-up on her. At first, she looked strange and felt out of place but soon got used to her different appearance. None of her Amish community would recognize her when she was dressed and made-up for a shoot. She felt free and no longer invisible. She felt important. She felt like *somebody*.

But now, her absence had been noticed. Amos paid more attention than the others. Part of her liked that someone in her Amish community finally noticed, but he could become a problem if he truly did keep her from leaving for her job. It was her job. An unusual job for an Amish person, true. For her, it was a dangerous job. How ridiculous. She didn't hurt anyone. No one would hurt her. But still, it was a secret. She certainly couldn't tell Amos where she went. But how many times could she claim to go for a walk and have him still believe her? Or worse yet, ask to go with her?

If she *were* going for a simple walk, she would welcome his company and attention. She smiled at the thought.

She sighed. That could never happen. She needed to figure something out before her next photo shoot.

COURTING HER SECRET HEART *by Mary Davis,
available September 2018 wherever
Love Inspired books and ebooks are sold.
www.LoveInspired.com*

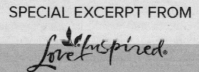
Amos Burkholder looked out over the Millers' fields to be plowed in the spring. He couldn't help but think of them as partly his. Of course, they weren't his fields, and he might not even be here to do the plowing and the planting. But if he was, he would take pride in that work.

Bartholomew Miller appreciated everything he did around the farm, so Amos worked harder than he ever had at home.

Bartholomew had never had a son to help him with all the work around the farm. How had he run this place without sons?

But on the flip side, Amos's *mutter* had been alone doing the house chores, cooking, cleaning and laundry for six men. How did she do it without help?

On the far side of one of the fields, a woman emerged from a bare stand of sycamore trees nestled next to a pond. She walked across the field.

The woman came closer and closer.

Deborah.

Where did she go all the time? She had disappeared every day this week and would be gone for hours. He was about to find out.

With her head down, she didn't see him approaching. He stepped directly into her path a few yards in front of her. When it looked as though she might literally run into him, he cleared his throat.

She halted a foot away. She was so startled to see him there, she appeared to lose her balance. Her arms swung out to keep herself upright.

He reached out and took hold of her upper arms to stop her from tumbling to the ground. "Whoa, there."

She gasped. "I'm sorry. I didn't see you."

"Where have you been all day?"

"What? Nowhere." She tried to pull free of his grip, but he held fast.

He shook his head. "You've been somewhere. You've left every day this week and been gone for most of the day."

"I—I went for a walk."

"Where? Ohio?"

"We have a pond just over there. I like to sit and watch the ducks. It's a nice place to think and be alone. You should go some time."

"I did. Today. You weren't there."

Her self-satisfied expression fell. "I was for a while, then I walked farther."

He sensed there was more to her absence than a walk. "Where?"

"Why do you care?"

"With your *vater* laid up, I'm responsible for everyone on this farm."

"I'm fine. I can take care of myself. May I go now?"

He didn't want to let her go but did. "I don't want you to leave the farm without telling me where you're going."

"Are you serious?"

He gave her his serious look.

She huffed and strode away.

Where did she go every day? He had wanted to follow her, but he realized it was none of his business. But curiosity pushed hard on him. He still might follow her if she didn't obey. Just to see. Just to watch her from a distance. Just to know her secret.

Something inside him feared for her. Feared she would walk out across this field and never return. Feared her secret would consume them both. She was a mystery.

A mystery he was drawn to solve.

*

Deborah heaved a sigh of relief. She marched the rest of the way through the field. After two weeks, Amos Burkholder already paid more attention to her comings and goings than her own family had her whole life—they thought her an airhead. Fanciful. Her head full of dreams and nonsense.

Well, she did have dreams. And to prove to everyone that she was someone to be noticed, she'd become a church member younger than any of her older sisters, at age sixteen. She'd basically skipped her Rumspringa.

No one had congratulated her or told her how wonderful it was that she'd joined so young. Anything to be noticed, just once.

Wasn't she as important as any of her sisters? Wasn't she just as much in need of being noticed?

So, she started taking advantage of her invisibility. Experimenting with being gone from the family for longer and longer periods of time, until she could be gone all day without hardly a word. She would claim to go for a walk and be gone for hours. When she returned home, she would be told to get her head out of the clouds and keep track of time.

But they never came looking for her.

So, Deborah wandered farther and farther from home. Until she'd ended up at the edge of a photo shoot over a year ago.

The photographer, Hudson, had seen her and said she'd be perfect for the shot. She hadn't wanted to do it. She knew she shouldn't. Hudson told her that there would be no harm in it. That no one would ever know.

She'd been thrilled at the idea of being special, being different. At being noticed. At no longer being invisible.

Hudson praised her and told her that she was a natural. He'd asked her to come to another shoot the following week. Soon, she participated in weekly shoots with him. And she had enjoyed it. She wasn't hurting anyone and was earning money for her future.

She felt free and no longer invisible. She felt important. She felt like somebody.

But now her absence had been noticed. She certainly couldn't tell Amos where she went. But how many times could she claim to go for a walk and have him still believe her? Or worse yet, ask to go with her?

If she had been going for a simple walk, she would welcome his company and attention. She smiled at the thought.

She sighed. That could never happen. She needed to figure something out before her next photo shoot.

Don't miss
Courting Her Secret Heart *by Mary Davis,*
available September 2018 wherever
Love Inspired® *books and ebooks are sold.*

www.Harlequin.com

Love Inspired®

Save $1.00

on the purchase of ANY

Love Inspired® book.

Available wherever books are sold,
including most bookstores, supermarkets,
drugstores and discount stores.

✄

Save $1.00

on the purchase of ANY Love Inspired® book.

Coupon valid until October 31, 2018.
Redeemable at participating retail outlets in the U.S. and Canada only.
Limit one coupon per customer.

52615841

Canadian Retailers: Harlequin Enterprises Limited will pay the face value of this coupon plus 10.25¢ if submitted by customer for this product only. Any other use constitutes fraud. Coupon is nonassignable. Void if taxed, prohibited or restricted by law. Consumer must pay any government taxes. Void if copied. Inmar Promotional Services ("IPS") customers submit coupons and proof of sales to Harlequin Enterprises Limited, P.O. Box 31000, Scarborough, ON M1R 0E7, Canada. Non-IPS retailer—for reimbursement submit coupons and proof of sales directly to Harlequin Enterprises Limited, Retail Marketing Department, 22 Adelaide St. West, 40th Floor, Toronto, Ontario M5H 4E3, Canada.

5 65373 00076 2 (8100)0 12374

U.S. Retailers: Harlequin Enterprises Limited will pay the face value of this coupon plus 8¢ if submitted by customer for this product only. Any other use constitutes fraud. Coupon is nonassignable. Void if taxed, prohibited or restricted by law. Consumer must pay any government taxes. Void if copied. For reimbursement submit coupons and proof of sales directly to Harlequin Enterprises, Ltd 482, NCH Marketing Services, P.O. Box 880001, El Paso, TX 88588-0001, U.S.A. Cash value 1/100 cents.

LICOUP00600

Looking for inspiration in tales
of hope, faith and heartfelt romance?

Check out **Love Inspired®** and
Love Inspired® Suspense books!

New books available every month!

CONNECT WITH US AT:

Harlequin.com/Community

 Facebook.com/HarlequinBooks

Twitter.com/HarlequinBooks

 Instagram.com/HarlequinBooks

Pinterest.com/HarlequinBooks

ReaderService.com

LIGENRE2018